As an assassin for the Dark Fae, Xanthe always wore a mask, hiding her emotions to do her duty. But when her identity is compromised, she trades undercover work for guarding Queen Niniane—a position that often brings her in contact with Chancellor Aubrey Riordan.

A year ago Aubrey's wife tried to assassinate their new queen in his name, a betrayal of everything he believes in. And now an attack on his life proves the dark conspiracy is not yet over. Although injured and weak, Aubrey can't help but be drawn to the shy assassin and loyal protector to the queen. Xanthe is everything Naida wasn't, and the passion she stirs in him is something he thought had long passed him by.

Hunter's Season

Thea Harrison

Hunter's Season
Copyright © 2012 by Teddy Harrison LLC
ISBN 13: 978-1-947046-96-2
Print Edition

Cover Photo-illustration © Kanaxa

This title was previously published and is being rereleased by the author. It has not been revised.

Dedication

I loved writing Hunter's Season for several reasons. In it I was able to wrap up the story arc of the mysterious Elder Races Tarot deck, and I was also able to, at long last, return to the Dark Fae land of Adriyel to catch up a little with Tiago and Niniane, the hero and heroine from *Storm's Heart.* This story also gave me the chance to give two very deserving people, Aubrey and Xanthe, a HEA (happily ever after) ending after their long, hard journeys.

You will also find a small HEA for a cameo character, a six year old Wyr housecat nicknamed Mouse, who has had her own rough journey. This character was the creation of the winner of my "Create an Elder Races Character" contest, in which many of you entered wonderfully creative inventions. I had huge fun taking the details of this small character and weaving them into the story, and I hope you have just as much fun reading about her.

Because of your enthusiasm and continued interest, I would love to dedicate this story to you, the readers.

Thank you so very much.

Wishing you many hours of happy reading,
Thea

Chapter One

Hearth

AS SOON AS XANTHE reached Adriyel, she left her mount at the palace stable and sent a message to Her Majesty's Chief of Security that said: "It is done."

Xanthe did not sign the note. He would know who had sent it. She did not expect a quick response either. With the completion of her assignment, any urgency or need for action had ceased.

Because she had been gone to America for some time, she stopped at the marketplace to buy food: fresh bread, meat, eggs, vegetables and fruit. The familiarity of the task soothed nerves that were tired and stressed from living with too much strangeness and danger for so long.

At midafternoon, the best of the goods had already been picked over, but there was still enough variety to meet her immediate needs. The market stalls were stocked with meat and fish, vegetables, fruit and grains from nearby farms, a variety of cooked foods, beautiful cloths of rich colors and intricate needlework, pottery, spices, soaps and metal work, and the recent, jarring addition of American goods. Hawkers called their wares, and the smells of cooking food wafted along the narrow cobblestone streets.

Xanthe paused as the small creature she carried in her pack stirred. A small creature might be too hungry to wait until she had cooked supper. After a moment's thought, she backtracked to the baker's stall to buy a meat pie. Her last purchase was an earthenware jug of fresh milk and a small tub of soft cheese. When she had finished the milk and the cheese, she would return the jug and the tub to the dairyman.

The wriggling in her pack became more urgent.

"Patience," she said to it.

Then she walked out of the city, down the narrow road that hugged the river for a couple of miles to the overgrown path that led to the small two-room cottage that had been her home for her entire life. Ignoring the increasingly strong wriggles in the pack on her back, she studied the cottage as she approached. It had a neglected air about it, as well it should, since she had been gone for over four seasons, but the roof looked solid enough. It led her to hope that the inside was dry.

She opened the door and looked into the shadowed, dusty interior. For a moment, it all looked too rustic, small and strange. Then the strangeness of the last several moons—months, they were called in America—fell from her eyes, and the cottage became once again as familiar to her as the back of her own hand, and she was home.

She remembered something a human had once said to her while she had been in the strange tent city at Devil's Gate in the American state named Nevada. The human had been sunburned and had worn a cynical expression when he said, "You know how that old saying goes—you can't go home again."

Xanthe had never been to America before, and she didn't know how the saying went. She wasn't sure what the human had meant.

She eased her packages onto the dusty table, shrugged out of her pack and set it carefully on the floor, and took off the shoulder harness that carried her sword, straightening tired shoulders. The day had already been full of travel, and there was still much to do before she could rest that night.

She propped the door open to the fresh, cooling air of the evening. Now the small creature in her pack was voicing shrill unhappiness. It sounded like a crying baby. She opened the pack and pulled out a thin, wriggling orange striped kitten that leaped out of her hands onto the table and circled the wrapped meat pie and dairy, meowing piteously.

"Yes, I know," Xanthe told it. "But you must wait a moment or two longer."

She had fallen into the habit of talking to the kitten on the trip from the crossover passage to Adriyel. They had developed a habit of sorts in the evenings on the short three day journey—the kitten would fall asleep, purring, either on her lap or beside the campfire while

Xanthe studied the lovely hand painted cards of the Tarot deck she had been given by a Vampyre and two medusae on her trip to Chicago, to the crossover passageway that led back home.

People in America had such an odd term for places like Adriyel. They called them Other lands, but to Xanthe, America was the Other land.

Most of the time the kitten seemed to enjoy the sound of her voice, but it wasn't interested in conversation at the moment. It swatted at the pie and meowed again, showing slender sharp white teeth and a tiny pink tongue.

Xanthe checked the cupboard that held the crockery. Along with all the other furniture in the cottage, her father had built the cupboard well out of hard seasoned wood. No small creatures had taken up residence in it, so she wiped out a bowl with the bottom of her sleeve, poured some milk into it and set it on the floor.

As the purring kitten leaped down and began to lap at the creamy liquid, she unwrapped and broke open the meat pie. It was still hot. Fragrant steam rose from the middle. She scraped meat and gravy onto a dish, blew on it until it had cooled slightly and set it on the floor by the bowl of milk.

While the kitten gorged itself on supper, Xanthe set to work. She dusted and swept out spiders and a few mice nests. With the kitten as a mouser, they wouldn't be back. Then she brought in half rotted wood from the small pile left under the lean-to, started a fire, uncovered the well and drew water, diced the raw meat and vegetables into a pot and set it over the fire to cook, washed the table and chairs, dragged the mattress out of the simple bedroom and beat it until the clouds of dust stopped rising, dragged it back inside and unpacked the linens and blankets that had been stored with fragrant cedar chips in a chest.

Her earlier tiredness was rapidly turning to exhaustion. She could have stayed in the city overnight and faced the long neglected cottage in the morning, but she had been too anxious to return to wait. After making the bed, she checked the bubbling pot that hung over the fire. Her mind was filled with visions of how pleasurable it would be to eat a hot bowl of stew and fall into the bed, when a gigantic shadow darkened her doorway.

The kitten shot past her feet, looking panicked, all its fur standing straight up. Xanthe raised her eyebrows as she turned to watch it race into the bedroom. It disappeared under the bed.

Then she turned to the doorway where a massive dark man stood, dressed in severe black. It was the Dark Fae Queen's chief of security, Lord Tiago Black Eagle, thunderbird Wyr and forever alien in the heartland of the Dark Fae.

Surprised, she bowed to her employer. "Welcome, my lord. Please do come in."

His features were as severe as his clothing. He looked foreign to eyes that were used to the slim build, large gray eyes and pale skin of the Dark Fae, but Xanthe had since gotten used to his harsh face and imposing demeanor.

Obsidian eyes narrowed as he stared in the direction of the kitten also. "Tenanye," he said, greeting her in that abrupt way of his that no longer seemed quite so odd after her sojourn in America. "I believe I told you to stop calling me that. Tiago will do just fine. What the hell is that doing here?"

She raised her eyebrows again as he gestured to the bedroom. "The kitten?" she asked. "I found it wandering the grounds on the other side of the crossover passageway in Chicago, so I brought it with me."

The crossover passageway from Adriyel to Chicago was located on an eighty-acre tract of land just northwest of the Chicago's downtown Loop area. The grounds held a large Georgian style mansion and were bordered by a tall stone wall that was topped with rolls of barbed wire, but the front gates were made of wrought iron and since Adriyel had opened its borders, more often than not, now those gates stood open.

None of the Dark Fae staff at the mansion would adopt a companion animal, but along with giving open access to other creatures, there was more than enough opportunity for urban wildlife to take advantage of the open gates and slip into the large, wooded area.

Tiago gave her a strange look then brushed past her to stride into the bedroom. "Come out from under there," he said firmly.

Xanthe stared at him, her tired mind blank with

astonishment.

The kitten slunk out from underneath the bed. It seemed even tinier and more delicate as it hunched at the Wyr lord's feet.

A wave of heat prickled Xanthe's skin as horrified comprehension began to dawn.

Tiago looked down at the small creature, hands on his hips. It stared up at him, still looking panicked, eyes completely round and fur bristling.

He ordered, "Change."

The kitten shapeshifted and became a dirty, unkempt girl who stared, seemingly mesmerized at the immense male in front of her. Tiago angled his jaw out and tilted his head at Xanthe.

Xanthe rubbed her forehead, her shoulders slumped. "Oh, gods," she said. "I kidnapped a little Wyr girl."

"She never once changed in front of you?" Tiago asked.

"No, sir. I had no idea. You know my magic sense is minimal." Xanthe had telepathy and the ability to traverse crossover passageways. She could also sense some Power in strong items and individuals, but without a Wyr's sense of smell, she hadn't any way to tell that the kitten was anything but what it seemed. She lifted her shoulders. "I thought I was rescuing a feral cat."

"Well," Tiago said after a moment. "I'll take her back to the palace with me. Niniane will know how to take care of this." He shot a look at Xanthe. "As for you, I will be in touch. I want to hear details about what happened."

"Understood, my l—sir," Xanthe said.

The little girl tore her gaze away from the towering figure in front of her to look at Xanthe. She whispered, "I want to stay here."

Immediately and in unison, Xanthe and Tiago said, "That can't happen."

"You named me Mouse," the girl said, her gaze pleading with Xanthe. "I was going to live in the cottage with you and be your mouser. You said so."

The plea tugged at Xanthe's heart. She thought of the kitten, curled on her lap and purring as she talked idly to it. She honestly could not remember all the things she had said. She walked over to squat in front of the child.

"That was when I thought you were just a cat," Xanthe told her softly. "While I would love for you to stay, I have no way to take care of a Wyr child." She had no way to take care of any child. Her life was too dangerous.

"But I like it here," the girl said plaintively. "I wouldn't be any trouble. I can be a cat all the time."

"I'm sorry, no," Xanthe said as gently as she could. She touched the girl's matted hair. "This place would not be good for you, darling. You deserve a much better place, where you can be both a cat and a little girl and go to school."

Tiago didn't wait for any more protestations. He scooped the girl up and turned toward the doorway. He said over one broad shoulder, "Relax and take some time for yourself. You've earned it. I'll send for you in the next day or two. Be ready."

"Yes, sir," Xanthe said.

Then he strode out the door. The last thing Xanthe saw of the girl were large sad eyes peering around the Wyr lord's shoulder.

Xanthe walked over to the sit at the table and rub her face. She would not reconsider as those large sad eyes had asked her to do. She could not.

Silence settled in the cottage. It seemed so much emptier than it had before Tiago had come. She stared at the items on the table that she had unloaded from her pack. There were various toiletries, weapons—her shoulder harness and sword, along with throwing knives—and the old, hand painted wooden box that held the Tarot deck.

The last of her energy had slipped away. She would put the things away tomorrow. For now, she pulled the box to her, opened it and pulled out the Tarot deck. Warm, mellow Power filled her hands as she reverently fingered the hand-painted cards.

She shuffled the deck and turned over the top card. It was one of the Major Arcana, Inanna, goddess of love, her chariot drawn by seven lions.

Inanna's card had been showing up every time she shuffled the cards.

"I thought you meant the cat," she said to the card.

The face of a golden woman smiled out at her, fierce

and mysterious.

She sighed. Love came in many forms—the love of a friend or lover, a parent or child. The devotion of a pet, or the love of one's country. Xanthe was really suited for only one of those, although for a while she thought the kitten might work.

She put the deck in the box and set it gently on the fireplace mantle. Then she ate some stew and fell into bed.

THE SUMMONS FROM the palace came early the next morning.

Everything was blanketed in light dew, and the tip of the sun barely showed through the trees. Xanthe had made a cup of tea and had taken it out to sit on an overturned log, enjoying the silence and the solitude.

It was peaceful at the cottage, with bright trills from birds and the rustle of wind blowing through the long grasses. She had never grown accustomed to the sounds and smells of American traffic, and for so long she had been unable to take much time to herself. She had always been surrounded by others she couldn't trust. It was exotic and liberating to feel the inner coil of tension that had been wound so tightly relax at last.

She heard the horseman on the path before she saw him, and the coil came back, tightening her stomach muscles. She stood and waited, and a few moments later, a palace guard trotted into view, leading another saddled, riderless horse. The guard didn't bother to dismount as he came up to her. Instead, he handed her a sealed note and the reins for the second horse, turned and left.

The note was a single word written in strong black slashes: "Come."

She blew out a breath. So much for relaxing and taking time for herself. After tethering the horse, she washed, dressed in her own palace black uniform, braided her silky hair and checked her appearance in the oval silver mirror in the bedroom.

Somewhere in the distant past, she had an ancestor who had not been Dark Fae and it showed in small ways. She was slim with an upright carriage, but her eyes were a darker gray than most Dark Fae's were. There was a sprinkle of light freckles across the bridge of her nose and along her cheeks, and her features were not quite as angular, her lips plump and curving. For those of the nobility who were concerned with the purity of breeding lines, those small differences were as good as a shout

Not that she was likely to try to pass herself off as noble any time in the foreseeable future. She tilted her head to check that her braid was neat, then she slipped on her shoulder harness that settled her sword onto her back, spread soft cheese over a slice of bread to eat on the journey and she shut the door gently as she left the cottage.

Adriyel was not a large city by American standards, but it was beautiful and busy. Her uniform and the horse created an open path for her on the cobblestone streets as people moved to make way for her. The buildings nestled harmoniously among the trees, and there was a long waterfront park by the river near the falls. As she approached the palace, she studied it with a critical eye.

Age and simple elegance defined the palace's architecture. The building was superbly designed and proportioned, the lines deceptively simple, yet phantoms lingered in Xanthe's mind whenever she looked at it, phantoms of blood and battle and screams in the night. Brushing them aside had long ago become habit. She took the horse to the stables and entered the palace through the servant's quarters.

The Wyr lord was in the Queen's private apartment. The two guards at the doors nodded respectfully to her and stood aside. "You're to go right in, ma'am," said the one on the right. If she remembered correctly, Rickart was his name.

"Thank you," she said. She shrugged out of her shoulder harness and handed her sword to him. One did not go armed into the Queen's presence unless expressly invited to do so.

Xanthe had only been in the Queen's apartment once before, and that had been seasons ago when the Queen and her Wyr lord had made the final decision on Xanthe's mission, so she looked around curiously as she entered. The rest of the interior of the palace was like the exterior, spacious and deceptively simple, sparely decorated with pieces of furniture, tapestries and sculptures that were national treasures.

The Queen's private apartment was another matter.

In the large sitting room color was splashed everywhere. Traditional embroidered tapestries covered the walls, and bowls and vases of flowers brightened dark polished wood surfaces. Red velvet couches were arranged in front of a fireplace and piled with pillows that were also embroidered with rich gold accents. An intricately carved bowl made of some lovely, translucent green stone Xanthe wasn't familiar with held miniature Reese's peanut butter cups. A scatter of books had been left carelessly on one table. Xanthe glanced at the haphazard pile. Dark Fae books on history and politics were intermingled with American mass market paperbacks, most of them romances.

Across the room, doors had been propped open to the sunny morning. They led to the terrace that looked out over the Queen's private walled garden. Hearing male voices outside, she walked over to the doors and looked out.

The Wyr lord sat at table, chatting easily with another tall figure of a man who was, by weight of his office alone, imposing in his own right. Chancellor Aubrey Riordan was one of the triad that formed the Dark Fae government, along with the Queen and the Commander of the Dark Fae army, Fafnir Orin. The Chancellor lounged in his chair facing the morning sun as he cradled a steaming cup of tea.

There was absolutely no question of Riordan's pure Dark Fae blood. He had strong, intelligent patrician features and light gray eyes that shone like clear water in sunlight. His long raven hair was bound back in a simple queue and gleamed blue-black in the bright light, his pointed ears elegantly shaped.

In contrast to his hair, his skin was ivory pale. While he did not have the Wyr lord's outsized physique, his long lean frame was muscled with graceful power. His eyes were narrowed in the sunlight, which revealed crow's feet at their corners, and a few strands of white hair gleamed at his temples. Riordan was not a young Fae, but a male in his full maturity of Power.

As she saw him, a sweet pain like a stiletto coated in honey slipped between Xanthe's ribs and pierced her heart. It was the same pain she always felt whenever she saw him. Like a silly child with her toys, for years she had gathered the snippets she heard about his life and hoarded them close.

Servants always knew the truth about their masters' true nature. What all the servants said about Riordan was that he was kind and even tempered. He never expressed frustration with a blow or a harsh word. One of the most powerful men in Adriyel, he held onto that power lightly and used it with care. For someone like Xanthe, who had rarely known kindness, he sounded as foreign and exotic as the Wyr lord who now kept him company.

The events of the last year had been cataclysmic for the Dark Fae, and also for Riordan himself. The despot Dark Fae King Urien had been killed by Dragos Cuelebre, the Lord of the Wyr, and with his death, at first it seemed there was no clear heir to the throne. For a short time, it had been whispered that Riordan, who was a distant relative in the Lorelle line, might be crowned king.

Then Niniane Lorelle, the true heir and Urien's niece, came out of hiding. She had been living in America ever since Urien and a handful of nobles had killed her father, King Rhian, and the rest of her family in a bloody palace coup.

Riordan had been married then, to a noble woman named Naida who had not accepted Niniane's claim to the throne, and who had tried a couple of times to have her assassinated. Instead Naida herself had been killed and her coconspirators incarcerated when the plot had been uncovered.

When that had happened something light inside of Riordan had darkened. Xanthe had seen it whenever she caught a glimpse of him on the palace grounds. He looked set, withdrawn, the expression in his gaze bleak and bitter. Whenever she thought of what his wife had done, she felt a useless fury at the woman who had been a traitor and a killer, and who with her actions had wounded such a decent man.

The moment Xanthe appeared in the doorway, Tiago turned his head and so did Riordan. She dropped her gaze. "My lords."

"There you are," said Tiago. "You must have gotten my message just after dawn." He put a booted foot on one chair and pushed it outward in her direction. "Sit and eat. Niniane will join us shortly."

Disconcerted, she lowered her head. "Thank you, my l—sir. That's very good of you, but I couldn't do that."

"Oh, you Fae and your social rules," said Tiago. He sounded exasperated. "Get over yourself, soldier. Plant your ass down here and eat some breakfast. That's an order."

Startled, her head came up. Before she could help herself, she looked at Riordan.

He smiled at her, his expression warm, and gestured to the chair Tiago had pushed out from the table. "You heard your employer," said the Chancellor. "Sit and help yourself to some food."

She couldn't help but stare. He looked different somehow than he had before she had left, less bitter in repose. Perhaps time was healing the wound that his wife had dealt him.

She took a deep breath and walked over to sit gingerly. She kept her gaze on her task as she did as she was ordered and helped herself to some of the breakfast on the table. There were boiled eggs, honey and berry pastries, fresh fruit and grilled venison. The bread and cheese she had eaten earlier seemed to have vanished completely, and her stomach rumbled. She tightened the muscles in her abdomen, hoping nobody had noticed.

She started to eat, and the two men resumed talking as if she wasn't there.

"You should have mentioned something about the lawsuit sooner," Tiago said.

After a slight hesitation, Riordan said, "I disagree. It's

my issue to resolve. At any rate, nothing will happen in a hurry. The suit will likely drag on for years."

Everything in Xanthe went quiet. Riordan was involved in some kind of legal dispute? It was news to her, so it must have happened while she had been away. Unwilling to show any reaction to what was obviously none of her business, she had to make a conscious decision to keep eating as she listened.

"There's no merit in the accusations," said Tiago. "You had no knowledge of what Naida was doing, and you weren't involved."

Riordan said cynically, "It doesn't matter whether or not we know that the case has any merit. The pursuant always has plenty of time to present their case and whatever they claim as true findings. That's simply how the Dark Fae justice system works. What you and Niniane achieved when you tried and executed the conspirators involved in the coup that killed her family was highly unusual, and that was because it involved the Queen herself, imprisonment of powerful nobility, and high treason."

"Naida's family is claiming you were treasonous," Tiago said.

"Not quite treason, in the legal sense," said Riordan. "Niniane had not yet been crowned. The best they can hope for is a charge of conspiracy. Since I was so much older than Naida and she was so young when we married, and all of Naida's crimes were supposedly on my behalf, they're claiming that I exerted 'undue influence' over her. Anyway, as you know only the government can instigate criminal cases. Since this is a personal suit and not an affair of the crown, the only thing they can hope to gain is monetary compensation."

"So they're being greedy," said Tiago after a moment.

"Yes," said Riordan flatly. "And to be brutally fair, they're also angry and they've suffered a loss, not only in terms of family but also their reputation."

"Well, the person they should be angry with is dead, and there isn't any evidence you had anything to do with it. I had you investigated myself."

"Of course you did," said Riordan. "I would have had me investigated as well."

Xanthe swallowed carefully, the food threatening to lodge in her throat. As she hadn't been involved in any investigating, that was more news to her. But as she considered it, she couldn't say she was surprised.

The Queen meant the world to the Wyr lord, and he was one of the most dangerous men she had ever met. He would have left no stone unturned in his investigation of Riordan. Even if he had not found any evidence, if he had the slightest suspicion that Riordan might have been involved in something that could potentially harm the Queen, Riordan would have been a dead man.

Having just killed a man herself on the Wyr lord's orders, she should know.

Chapter Two

Law

AT FIRST THE silent woman in the soldier's uniform hadn't interested Aubrey, other than he took note of how openly Tiago talked in front of her.

Although Tiago and Niniane never flaunted anything in public, they were a love match. The Wyr was obsessed with anything to do with his mate, and her safety and wellbeing. If Tiago relaxed and talked in front of this woman, then Aubrey could too.

Gradually, though, the woman's very silence drew Aubrey's attention. He glanced at her from time to time, noting various details, how precisely and smoothly she cut her food, the utter expressionlessness in her face, how she never looked up once from her meal. She embodied polite distance, her entire demeanor proclaiming that an invisible wall existed between her and the two men.

A patter of quick, light footsteps sounded on the terrace flagstones, and Tiago's harsh, forbidding features lit up. The woman shot to her feet and stood at attention. Aubrey and Tiago stood at a more leisurely pace as Niniane Lorelle, the Dark Fae Queen swept into their presence, chatting as she came toward them.

"Sorry I am late—oh good, you didn't wait for me. Good morning, Aubrey."

"Good morning, my dear." He bent his head to receive Niniane's kiss on the cheek.

She was dressed for personal comfort rather than for state, in simple dark tunic and leggings. She was dainty in every way, and while she wasn't precisely beautiful, she had a warmth and effervescence that could always banish the darkness in Aubrey's soul, at least for a while. She was the child of his long dead friends, and the only Lorelle left alive, and he had grown to love her like he would if she were his own daughter.

Still talking, she moved around the table to Tiago. "Hello, darling." Niniane lifted her face for Tiago's kiss, which he delivered to her mouth with relish. "I've just come from the nursery. I wanted to check on the girl. She is adorable, but she still won't say anything about where she came from or who she really is, and she insists that her name is Mouse."

"At least she's talking to you and the nurse," said Tiago. "She wouldn't say a word to me. I frightened her too much."

Niniane gave him a wry grimace. "The nearest I can tell, she has got to be around six years old. Given how ingrained the dirt was on her, and how matted her hair, I think it's possible she might have lived on the streets for some time. If that's the case, I think she might have changed into her cat form and stayed that way to survive. I sent someone this morning to Chicago to do some investigating. For all we know, there might be pictures of her on milk cartons." Her expression turned troubled. "I suppose we shouldn't keep her, should we?"

Tiago shook his head, his face gentling. "No, faerie. It would not be fair to a young Wyr to be fostered among the Dark Fae. Housecat Wyr have life spans akin to humans. That would not matter at first, but eventually she would grow old while everyone she grew to care about would not. She needs a good home with her own kind."

Niniane's shoulders drooped. "I knew that," she muttered. "I just needed to hear you say it to me."

As the two talked, Aubrey glanced at the soldier again. Hands tucked behind her back, she regarded her half eaten plate of food as though it was the only thing in the world of interest to her. A corner of Aubrey's mouth lifted. She was really quite good.

"Sit down," said Tiago. "I'll order fresh tea and hot food for you."

"No, don't bother," said Niniane. "This is all fine." She turned to face the silent woman with a friendly grin. "So you're the one who kidnapped a little Wyr girl?"

The woman's façade broke. She moved, looked up and took in a deep breath as color flooded her skin, and after such a long display of perfect, polite disinterest, the look of dismay on her face startled a quiet chuckle out of

Aubrey.

"Yes, your grace, I am," said the woman. "I am terribly sorry."

She looked more than sorry; she looked so mortified even Tiago grinned.

"Don't be," said Niniane. "Your 'kidnapping' might have saved her life." She sat and helped herself to breakfast while Tiago poured her a cup of tea. "What have I missed?"

Aubrey and Tiago sat too. The woman remained standing until Tiago shot her a frowning glance. Then she sat as well, although she did not touch any more of her food. Tiago said, "Aubrey and I were discussing a suit that Naida's family has filed against him."

"Yes, I learned of it this morning when my secretary briefed me," said the Queen, her voice turning cool. "I have already sent a dismissal to Justice Kellen for the court."

The woman's reactions, or lack of, had begun to fascinate Aubrey, so he was looking at her when Niniane spoke. He watched a subtle, strange expression flare in her dark gray eyes. Oddly, it appeared to be relief mingled with satisfaction, but he must be mistaken. Then the meaning of Niniane's words caught up with him, and he set his cup down gently as he turned to the Queen.

The monarchy had every right to dismiss cases and issue pardons, but in actuality this was done so rarely that the action carried a great deal of weight. The dismissal would be highly public by the end of the day and a great humiliation to Naida's family.

He said, "While I am both touched and honored by your show of faith, I had thought Naida's family's anger might run its course during the length of the suit."

Tiago said, much more bluntly, "Are you sure you want to do that, faerie?"

"Yes, I am quite sure," said Niniane. She snapped a delicate bite of food off of her fork then pointed her fork at Aubrey. "You are Chancellor by my appointment. Naida's attempt was on my life, and I assure you, we investigated that quite thoroughly. For months that was almost the only thing Tiago and I talked about, along with the investigation of Urien's conspirators."

"I can attest to that," Tiago said.

Niniane stabbed her fork in the air, eyes sparking with anger. "At best their case against you would have been full of supposition and resentment, and at worst, full of fabrication. That suit was not just a slap in the face to you, Aubrey. It was a slap in the face to me. I will not have my people harassed. I will not have my judgments questioned like that. The dismissal is the best thing that could have happened for them, because if they were allowed to continue and if they were foolish enough to present false evidence, I would order the courts to prosecute them. If they think their lives are ruined now, it would be nothing compared to what would happen to them then."

Silence fell over the table. Tiago's expression was filled with, yes, amusement and indulgence, but also genuine admiration and respect. The woman who was his soldier watched the Queen with sparkling eyes, while Niniane continued to point her fork at Aubrey, eyebrows raised.

Aubrey cleared his throat. "Since you put it that way, thank you for your championship."

She smiled at him. "You're welcome. Now, onto something else." She looked at the soldier sitting opposite her. "Your name is Xanthe, is that correct? Tiago tells me you have a tale to tell."

Aubrey watched the woman glance at him then at Tiago, who nodded. "Speak freely," he told her.

She nodded and took a breath. "My assignment has been completed. Cieran Thruvial is dead. He died in a place called Devil's Gate in Nevada, where we went after we had crossed over to America."

The place name was unfamiliar to Aubrey but he wasn't surprised at that. He watched as Niniane and Tiago gave each other a long look.

Tiago murmured, "It's finally done. The last of them have been brought to justice."

"We can look to the future now," Niniane said. They shared an intimate smile. Then Niniane turned back to Xanthe. "I've never heard of this place."

"Devil's Gate is new since your grace has come to Adriyel," said Xanthe. "A—a tent city, they call it, although many of the structures are not tents. Some are vehicles called RVs. Others are buildings they called Quonset and there are also temporary office spaces made of metal. Close to two hundred thousand people, both humankind and Elder Races, are there now looking for magic sensitive silver and gold."

"There's a modern day gold rush going on, and I didn't know anything about it?" Niniane sounded dismayed.

"You need more sleep than I do," Tiago said to her. "I've been following the stories in the newspapers."

Niniane muttered, "We have got to start spending some time each year in Chicago, especially now that we've opened our borders."

"Agreed," said Tiago. He told Xanthe, "Continue."

She said, "The place is—crowded and chaotic. Lord Thruvial thought he could relax in some relative anonymity there. He was well away from Adriyel's politics and the trials of all the other conspirators. He believed that since you could not find enough evidence of his involvement in the overthrow and murder of your father and family that he would not be pursued further."

Aubrey looked steadily across the table at the deadly face of the man who sat opposite him. Thruvial had not only been a pig, but an idiot.

Xanthe said, "Since I was the most junior of his triad, for a long time I was not allowed to perform any of the more intimate tasks of service to him, like serving him food and drink or helping him to dress."

"She was in his household for months," Tiago told Aubrey. "It never fails to surprise me how assholes like Thruvial insist on Dark Fae traditions like keeping triads of personal servants, but then they can turn around and murder their own king."

Triads were found throughout all aspects of the Dark Fae daily life, from the highest place in government to fighting formations and servant clusters. Often in society, married couples brought a third sex partner to the marriage bed, although Aubrey had never felt inclined to do so.

He gave Tiago a dark smile. "That is not inconsistent, my friend. Our traditions of violence, jealousy, revenge, and making and breaking political alliances, go deeper than any triad."

Tiago snorted. "Point." He said to Xanthe, "So Thruvial finally relaxed and let you get close enough."

"Yes, but even so, I had to wait for the right moment to act so that it could not be traced back to me. When the opportunity finally came, I poisoned his wine." Her voice was composed and steady. "He died quickly. Unfortunately that was not the end of it."

Aubrey settled back in his chair, watching her face as she told the story. There were odd, intriguing freckles, light like sprinkles of gold, on her nose and cheeks. Her eyes were unusual too, a deep, rich color full of shadows and mystery. Her face was gently planed, with high cheekbones and a narrow rounded jaw. Now that he came to really study her, he realized she had a shockingly sensual mouth. She would never be considered one of the high beauties of the Dark Fae, but she did have her own particular attractiveness.

"There was trouble?" Tiago asked.

"Yes. A young medusa also resided in Devil's Gate, and she was known to argue publicly with Lord Thruvial. When his other attendants found him poisoned, they started an outcry that ran through the camp. They insisted that she was the one who poisoned him, and she was taken and locked up to be hung." Her expression turned bitter. "The whole thing was entirely my fault. I did not consider all the ramifications of what might happen if I killed him in such a fashion. I simply saw my opportunity and took it."

Niniane leaned forward. "You can't consider how everybody might react to something. It's too much to ask of yourself."

Other than a quick glance at the Queen, Aubrey's gaze returned to Xanthe's face. He was interested to note that her self-recriminating expression hadn't changed even though the Queen herself offered absolution. This young soldier had a strong set of scruples.

He asked in a quiet voice, "Is the medusa girl all right?"

She turned to him quickly. "Yes, my lord. While I waited and watched for an opportunity to help, her aunt and a friend came. Together we were all able to get out." She looked at Tiago and Niniane. "You actually know them—it was Duncan Turner and Dr. Seremela Telemar."

Aubrey was acquainted with Duncan slightly, for he had met the young Vampyre when Niniane had travelled from Chicago to Adriyel for her coronation. Niniane had been accompanied by a Dark Fae delegation, along with the Vampyre Carling Severan, who had been a member of the Elder tribunal, and her attendants. Aubrey didn't know the physician, but it was clear from Tiago and Niniane's intense startlement that they knew both of the others.

"You already said that everybody is all right, but how are Duncan and Seremela?" Niniane asked. She sounded wistful. "I would love to see them again."

"They were quite well when I took my leave," Xanthe told her. "And so was Dr. Telemar's niece. They said to offer you their very best wishes."

Tiago nodded to her in approval. "Despite your misgivings, it sounds like all ended well."

She hesitated. "That's not all, sir."

Aubrey set his cup down as Tiago's eyes narrowed. "What is it?"

She straightened her knife in precise alignment with her fork, gaze focused on her hand, as she said, "Lord Thruvial's other two attendants caught up with us before we could get clear away. Duncan Turner and I had to kill them. The fight was not quiet, and there may have been witnesses. Before that point, I had declared publicly that I was in support of the young medusa's innocence." This time when she lifted her gaze, her expression was resigned. "I'm the only surviving member from Thruvial's household, and I disappeared right after his attendants were killed. For any particularly clever observer, it would not be hard to put two and two together, and there were any number of clever people at Devil's Gate. With information now flowing freely from America into Adriyel..." She let her voice trail away into silence.

Tiago folded his arms as he regarded her. "Your identity has been compromised. I cannot use you for other undercover assignments."

Xanthe's shoulders slumped. Even though she had been the one to bring the point up, Aubrey could see how clearly Tiago's words disappointed her. Something about it moved him. Loyalty and dedication were precious things, and hers showed in her eyes, shining straight like a sword.

He heard himself saying, "Do not distress yourself over this. Your service will not go unrewarded. You are too valuable of an asset to waste."

This time when she looked at him, she did not glance quickly and away. Instead she met and held his gaze. He found himself looking at her deeply. He did not know what he saw in her eyes—surprise? Gratitude? He did not know her well enough to read the nuances.

"I like her," Niniane said suddenly. Her voice broke the unexpected connection that had grown between them, and they both turned to her. The Queen rested her chin in one hand as she studied Xanthe. "She's discreet, she rescues kittens and she cares about the consequences of her actions." She said to Tiago, "I want her."

His expression turned indulgent. "If you want her,

you can have her."

"Well, thank you," Niniane said, "but I think we should consult with her about that." She turned back to Xanthe. "What do you think? Would you like to come work with me as one of my attendants? Please answer truthfully. I know guard duty isn't for everyone, and those who have been close to me in the last year have not fared very well." A shadow darkened her eyes, and Aubrey remembered the casualties from last year, a bright human woman named Cameron Rogers who died while saving Niniane's life, and Arethusa, the late Commander of the Dark Fae army.

As he thought of them, his heart felt as heavy as a stone, and as dead. So many deaths, so much grief, that Naida had caused.

Niniane shook herself visibly and continued. "Perhaps you are no longer interested in active duty or this position, so you won't hurt my feelings if you would rather not. We will make sure that you are placed in a position to which you are suited and that will make you happy."

Pleasure had lit Xanthe's expression, and in that moment she was truly beautiful. "I'm deeply honored, your grace, and I would love to work for you."

The shadows disappeared from Niniane's gaze, and she clapped her hands. "Oh goody!"

"I promised her time off first," Tiago said. "She's earned it."

"Of course she has," Niniane said. She asked

Xanthe, "How much time would you like?"

"Might I take a sevenday?" the other woman asked in a diffident tone.

"You have been gone for some time. You may take a month—I mean a moon—if you like," Niniane told her. "Are you sure a sevenday is sufficient?"

Xanthe nodded.

"Very well, come to me first thing on the eighth day." Niniane gestured to Xanthe's unfinished plate of food. "Have you had all that you want?"

"Yes, your grace."

"Then your vacation begins now. Thank you for telling us what happened, and enjoy your sevenday."

Xanthe stood, bowed deeply to Niniane, inclined her head at Tiago and Aubrey, and left.

Silence fell over the three who remained on the terrace, as Niniane resumed work on her breakfast and Tiago sank deep into his thoughts.

Aubrey finished his tea, his own thoughts turning dark as they always did anymore when he looked inward. He suspected that the most interesting part of his day had just taken her leave.

After Niniane finished her meal, she turned her attention to him and began asking questions. He had breakfast with Niniane a few times every sevenday, so that he could keep her abreast of the latest happenings in the congress and the courts. Sometimes Tiago joined them, and sometimes he didn't. After listening to their conversation for several minutes, Tiago excused himself.

The rest of Aubrey's schedule was filled with the never ending administrative part of his duties as Chancellor. He found himself wondering what the young soldier, Xanthe, was doing with the first of her sevenday, and how she was enjoying her time off. While she must have been around before on the extensive palace grounds, she would have been virtually anonymous among all of the black uniformed guards, and he had never noticed her before.

What would that quiet, reserved woman do for pleasure? Did she read, or work with metal, or garden or paint? After having been gone for so long, she must feel quite out of touch with her friends, if she had any. It was hard to maintain friendships when one worked as an agent for the crown.

As the afternoon faded to evening, his thoughts turned to Naida's family. The Ealdun family were minor nobility and much poorer than Aubrey. Naida's marriage to Aubrey had been advantageous to them in every way, and now they had not only lost that connection by marriage, but their daughter had been branded a traitor.

Aubrey hadn't minded either the social and financial differences, or the age difference, as Naida had been much younger than he. He had not loved Naida the way that Niniane and Tiago loved each other. He couldn't remember if he had ever hoped to find that kind of fierce, passionate love. If he had, it was lost in the distance of his long ago youth.

But he had known long, deeply caring liaisons with

many lovers, and he had enjoyed his marriage with Naida, enjoyed having her companionship in the daytime hours and in bed. She had been clever, strong minded, and quick to grasp political and social nuances, and she had been funny, her wit dry and often sardonic. He had loved and respected her, and had considered her a good partner and a friend.

He had trusted her.

What she had done had come as a raw shock. Her attempts to kill Niniane were not only a betrayal of the true heir, but most importantly, they were a betrayal of him. What she had done went against everything that Aubrey stood for and believed in, and if she had succeeded in killing Niniane, he knew that she would have never told him what she had done.

In the aftermath of her death, he doubted himself and his own judgment of people. He might have missed her, except when the shock and guilt eased enough for other feelings to come in, he felt so angry at her for what she had done. He wanted to shout at her and throw her out of the house, and he could do none of that because she was dead.

He had no idea how he would ever grow to trust someone again. He felt so angry all of the time, and bitter. He felt cheated. He understood how the Ealcuns might feel angry and cheated too.

How would they react to the news of the Queen's dismissal? He believed they would take it very badly and he braced himself for the possibility of ugly missives awaiting him when he arrived home, or even a confrontation in public or possible retaliation in another way.

They had already dropped out of social gatherings, and it would be some years before their reputation recovered enough for them to receive invitations again. Prosecuting him had been, among other things, a way for them to try to distance themselves from the stain of what Naida had done. They could have claimed horror and righteous indignation, and they must have hoped to turn censure away by pointing fingers at someone else, but now that avenue had been denied them.

He also understood Niniane's anger and the reasons for her dismissal of the Ealdun's lawsuit, but he could not help but wish it had been allowed to run its course.

For one thing, he had been most interested to find out what evidence the Ealdun s might offer up to the court as proof of his undue influence over Naida.

He had wanted to know just how far they would go for money, and for their pride.

Perhaps he could still find out. He sent for one of his junior secretaries, a steady, discreet fellow named Sebrin who had a very sharp mind. Once Sebrin had stepped inside his office, he nodded for the younger male to shut the door.

"You might have heard the news by now," he said. "The Queen has dismissed the Ealduns' lawsuit against me."

"Oh, very good, sir," said Sebrin, which did not

happen to confirm whether he had heard already or not.

Aubrey suppressed a smile. Discreet, indeed. He was pleased with his choice in hiring Sebrin. He said, "I want you to dig quietly into the details of that lawsuit. See if you discover what sort of evidence they claimed to have. I don't expect they would have had time to file anything detailed, so this will probably not be in court records. You may have to travel to the Ealdun's home seat." He paused. "Do you understand what I am asking you to do?"

He could see in the other man's intelligent expression that Sebrin understood him perfectly. "Yes, my lord."

"Do you have any problem with the assignment?"

"Not at all, my lord." Sebrin added emphasis to each word, his eyes sparkling. "I think it will be quite interesting."

"Very good. Be careful and keep your head down. That will be all." He sat back in his chair, his hands steepled together as he watched Sebrin bow and take his leave.

He wasn't sure what he would do with the answers when he received them, but it still felt good to take at least some kind of action. He hoped he would be wrong, but he fully expected to be incensed at whatever Sebrin might find. After all, the Ealduns would not have filed a lawsuit if they hadn't believed they could argue a case against him.

In the meantime, he would get nothing else

accomplished at work that day. As the sun dipped below the horizon, he finally sent his secretaries off. Then as was his habit, he walked the short distance along torch lit streets to the stylish neighborhood near the palace where his house was located.

It was an old and gracious building, and despite the triads of servants it held to fulfill his every whim, somehow it was still quite empty.

Chapter Three

Death

"IT'S THE QUEEN, isn't it?" Xanthe asked Inanna's card that night.

The love of one's country could certainly be personified as the love of one's Queen. This possibility fit even better than the kitten had.

The card, of course, made no comment. Divination came through Elder Tarot decks in ways other than outright language, depending on which card spread one laid. All the Major Arcana were the seven Elder gods, the primal Powers that moved and sustained the universe. Love, Death, Will, Law, The Depths, The Hearth. And the god who was god over all the others, The Dance.

All the Minor Arcana were the various aspects of each god. The nuances were in the combinations. Love and Death could mean grief or loss. Love and Will, which was sometimes known as The Gift, could mean sacrifice. The most accurate and comprehensive messages were found in a complete spread.

At least, that was true of a normal Tarot deck.

When she had traveled back from Devil's Gate to Chicago with Duncan Turner, Seremela Telemar and her niece, Xanthe had cheated.

Because Seremela was a physician with highly trained magical skills, the others had assumed that she was the expert when she examined the mysterious Tarot deck that her niece had stolen. And she was, mostly. All Xanthe had to do was remain silent while she watched and listened. She learned that despite Seremela's expertise, the physician couldn't identify what kind of Power infused the cards, or what the Power might mean, or how it might exert influence on the world around it.

Xanthe never told them that she knew how to lay a Tarot spread. She also never told them of the tiny suspicion that had been born as she listened to Seremela speculate. She simply took the opportunity to gain possession of the cards when it presented itself.

The others expected her to take the deck to Dark Fae elders and experts.

She might do that, eventually.

There were ancient shrines dotted throughout Adriyel, dedicated to each of the Elder gods. She might also take the deck to each of the shrines to see if something happened, although she had not decided about that. For now Seremela had said the Power in the deck had pulled to Xanthe, and so she honored the deck's wishes by keeping it.

The oldest of the old Dark Fae legends spoke of Powerful things that existed, put into the world by the gods to enact their will. If this was such an incredibly rare item, and if Xanthe had the knowledge, Power and skill with which to use it, she could come to rule the Dark Fae if she so wished.

If and if. For all their vast power, the gods could not take away a person's free will, and Xanthe did not so wish. Nor did she have the knowledge, Power or skill. She hadn't even gotten up the courage to actually lay out a complete spread, although she would one day soon.

For now she held the cards and shuffled them. She enjoyed the gentle, mellow feel of the Power that soaked into her hands as she handled them, and she liked to study the lovely hand-painted images while quiet whispers and vague images brushed along the edges of her mind.

And she took sober, respectful note of how Inanna's card continued to surface.

Part of why she lacked the courage to lay a complete spread was she did not want to witness an augury that was filled with sacrifice or grief. Instead, she liked to imagine that Inanna's card meant good things, light things.

Her long trip from home had been dark and violent. She had witnessed Thruvial and the others do things that turned her stomach and sickened her soul, and she had to do all of that with more than just an expressionless face. If she could not manage enjoyment, she had to at least feign support. She had not known from day to day if she would even survive the trip. There had been many nights when she would lie awake and wonder if she would die alone without friends.

Now, even if it was only for a little while, she needed to imagine those good, light things.

"You would not deny me that, would you?" she asked Inanna.

The woman on the card. She was so strong, so strong.

XANTHE SPENT HER sevenday working on the cottage, cutting and weeding away the long tangled foliage, arranging for wood to be delivered, and walking the short path to sit and dream by the Adriyel River. Sometimes she fished for her supper. Sometimes she waded in the shallows at the edge of the river where she had played as a child.

Sometimes she watched the river barges until the sun dropped low and shone a shimmering path on the dappled, mysterious surface, beckoning her to walk an impossible journey on the water into the light.

She spoke to as few people as possible and let the silence sink into her soul. It washed away some of the terrible stains, not all, but enough so that she did not lie awake at night, dwelling on thoughts of her own death.

On the eighth day, first thing in the morning, she presented herself at the palace to await the Queen's pleasure.

The Queen was very pleased indeed.

"Whee!" said Niniane, grinning widely as Xanthe

stepped into her apartment. "There you are! I'm so excited that you are here. Did you have a good time on your vacation? Did you get enough rest? I will be most unhappy if you ever try to fib to me because it is something you think I want to hear."

"I have rested quite well, thank you, your grace. I am excited and honored to be here."

Xanthe stood at rest, her hands clasped loosely behind her back as she regarded the smaller woman with some bemusement. Niniane was dressed in a pale pink, filmy wraparound robe that had a neckline and hem of floating, tiny feathers. She wore odd, dainty American shoes that matched, with high heels and a single strap that somehow held them onto her feet, and with more of the floating, tiny pink feathers along the strap. Her dark hair was pinned up, and somehow it looked both messy and softly feminine.

Niniane caught the direction of her gaze and held out a small foot. "This ridiculous floaty, feathery stuff is marabou, and I love it beyond all reason."

"It is certainly striking," Xanthe told her in perfect truthfulness.

The Queen giggled. "How precisely worded of you. You know, I am quite the proper Dark Fae Queen out there." She waved her hands in the general direction of the doors. "But in here, in private, I get to relax and be anything I want to be. The only thing is—" She looked around mournfully. "I don't have cable."

Xanthe blinked. "Then I shall fetch one for you

immediately. It would help for me to know what kind of cable you require."

Niniane giggled harder. "Oh no, I do not require that kind of cable. 'Cable' is slang for cable TV. I suppose in Thruvial's household, you did not have access to any television during your months in America?"

"Ah, no," said Xanthe. "However, we were able to examine a television in one of the motels we stayed in when we journeyed to Nevada." She paused then added delicately, "Watching this device seemed an odd pastime."

"Oh, it is," Niniane assured her. "It's also fun, if there is a good story to watch. Theoretically. In Cuelebre Tower in New York, the cable company was horrendous and installed everything wrong. Then they couldn't seem to get it fixed right until Dragos himself went to talk to the head of the company. After that, the problems were fixed within a week. All eighty floors." She heaved a sigh. "It must be good to be a dragon."

"One imagines so," said Xanthe politely.

She settled quickly into her new routine and duties, which were at times not at all what she had expected. The Queen had lived for two hundred years in New York, and while, as she had said, she maintained formality in public, in private she indulged in her odd, casual American ways. Often she and Tiago dined privately in her apartment. On the occasional nights when the Queen was not engaged, yet Tiago was away at work, Xanthe learned how to play card games called euchre and hearts, and once she endured a painfully long board game called Monopoly. She was not eager to repeat the experience.

She found that while she had taken her sevenday, investigators had discovered that the little Wyr girl's mother was a drug addict who was so far gone in her own mind, she hadn't noticed the child had been missing. The investigators had contacted other family members who, shocked to find out what had happened, had filed for emergency custody. As soon as they could arrange to do so, they would be traveling to Adriyel to collect the girl and bring her home. Niniane would provide financial help so that they could take time away from their jobs and make the journey. Xanthe was sorry to hear of the mother's neglect, but glad to know the child would go to a home where she would be cared for and she could belong.

On the days when she had early duty, afterward she traveled home to the cottage. When she had late duty, she stayed overnight in the palace barracks. Every sevenday she received her wages and she got not one but two full days off, a new policy which had been instituted by this Americanized Queen and felt like the height of luxury. She also received several moons pay that was owed to her for her assignment to infiltrate Thruvial's household and execute Tiago's kill order. For the first time in a very long time, she had a tidy nest egg that she could set aside and leave untouched.

On the one hand it felt good wear the palace black,

not to have to cover up her identity or put on a mask. On the other hand, there were times when the guard duty felt too passive. Fortunately the Queen was quite active. Due to Xanthe's senior status, she could have become captain of the Queen's personal guard, but that would have involved extra boring duties such as scheduling, and besides, Rickart was a good man and didn't deserve to be supplanted.

She saw Chancellor Riordan often, as much as several times a week. He and the Queen might take a walk through the palace grounds as they discussed an issue, or they shared breakfast. They often attended the same functions, whether it was a dinner of state, or some gala like the annual regatta, where boats and barges of all sizes and kinds floated on the river, lit with colored lanterns that reflected off the sparkling black water until the night was ablaze with light. During those occasions, Xanthe usually saw Riordan from a distance, although there were always the moments when he greeted Niniane. Then he would glance at Xanthe and smile.

She treasured those smiles. They were fleeting, and of course they meant nothing. They were just a courtesy, little more than a pat one might give a horse. But he looked right into her eyes when he smiled, and for the briefest moment, she felt outside of her life, transported somewhere else.

She had already devoted herself to the Queen when she went to work for Tiago. It was easy to grow fond of Niniane, who was funny, charming and kind to everybody, including her servants. But Xanthe would have taken the position as Queen's attendant solely for the chance of receiving one of those rare smiles from Riordan.

One night soon after the regatta, Niniane had just finished a dinner in the great hall with prominent American businessmen and a collective of Dark Fae artisans and metalworkers. Neither Riordan nor Tiago had attended. The palace was built on a hillside, and the great hall was on the lower level with massive windows that offered a spectacular view of the nearby falls and river.

The Americans were suitably impressed, and the Dark Fae artisans were frankly delighted. The results looked to be highly promising for a healthy increase in trade, but the affair had gone on overlong, and Xanthe was hot, tired and hungry. She had eaten a snack just before the dinner and a full meal would be waiting for her in the kitchen, but she was just as inclined to slap a piece of meat between two pieces of bread, go to her bed in the barrack and call an end to the day.

Niniane looked as tired as she felt. She gestured for one of the servers who came to her immediately. "Please let Lord Black Eagle know that the dinner is over, and I am retiring for the night."

"Yes, your grace." The server trotted away.

Niniane glanced at Xanthe and gave a ghost of a chuckle. "I enjoy dinners like this, but there's a limit to how many functions poor Tiago can endure, so I try not to ask too much of him."

Xanthe inclined her head. Also, she thought, the risk factor for this dinner had not been high. There was a distinct pattern to the lord's behavior. Anything to do with Dark Fae nobility or involving open air, like the regatta, and Tiago was sure to attend. He was also present for anything that Niniane particularly loved, such as going to a drama house to see any of the many plays that were dark, twisting tales filled with swordfights, deceit, treachery and impossible love. "Bloody soap operas," he called them, but he said it in that easygoing indulgent way of his that seemed for Niniane alone, and besides, Xanthe suspected that he enjoyed the plays too.

She and Niniane walked back to the Queen's apartment. They had climbed the grand staircase to the upper hall when she heard running footsteps behind them. All the blood in her body pounded. She shoved Niniane forward and drew her sword as she spun to meet the newcomer, because running at that urgent pace in the palace was never good.

She recognized the palace runner immediately and straightened out of attack position, although she did not sheathe her sword. The runner, a young girl named Drinde and unarmed, paused cautiously several steps below Xanthe and held onto the guard rail, gasping for breath. "Pardon, ma'am—your Highness. Oh, you must come quickly!"

Niniane had come up beside Xanthe, her face blanched white. In a harsh voice that sounded quite unlike her, she snapped, "What has happened?"

"It's Chancellor Riordan, your grace," Drinde stammered. "He has been attacked. His servants—his servants say it is very bad."

Xanthe's world gave an ugly, sickening lurch. Beside her, Niniane tore off the stiff, richly worked, knee length jacket she wore. The jacket was a work of art and highly restrictive. She threw it to the floor. Underneath it she wore a thin shirt made of fine cotton, leggings and polished ankle boots.

"Let's go," Niniane said.

Abruptly Xanthe's mind clicked over to icy logic that won control just barely over the hot panic galloping through her body. "We don't know the veracity of this. It might be a trap." She turned to Drinde. "Are you sure they were the Chancellor's servants?"

The girl met her gaze. "Yes, ma'am."

That meant nothing. It could still be a trap. Everything inside of her was screaming to race to Riordan's house. Instead, she forced herself to say to Niniane, "I have to advise you to wait until Tiago is found."

"Noted," the Queen said in a clipped tone. "We're not waiting. We'll collect guards on our way out." The Queen looked at Drinde. "Find Lord Black Eagle. Tell him what has happened, and where we have gone."

Niniane didn't wait to hear the girl's reply. She turned and raced down the hall, and Xanthe raced beside her. They burst through a set of doors, out into a warm, humid night. Xanthe shouted for guards and several came running. She asked Niniane, “A carriage?”

“It’s quicker on foot,” Niniane said. Her eyes were frightened and bleak.

Xanthe rapped out orders. The guards surrounded Niniane, and they all took off running, down the colonnade of ancient sycamores, along the stately mansions on Ambassador’s Row, cutting across a small park and then racing down that street to the end where the Chancellor’s house was ablaze with torchlight. All the while Xanthe remained at a razor’s edge, just this side of violence, her gaze darting around to every dark shadow and to the guards that surrounded her and the Queen, while her mind kept replaying those few, terrible words that Drinde had spoken.

“He has been attacked.”

Riordan was strong, and he would have access to some of the most highly skilled and Powerful physicians in Adriyel.

If the physicians could reach him in time.

“His servants say it is very bad.”

One of their guards raised his fist to pound at the front door of the Chancellor’s house, just as it opened. A distressed male servant looked out at them. His gaze landed on Niniane, and his face crumpled. “Your Majesty, this is so terrible—”

Niniane said through whitened lips, “Is he dead?”

“No, not—no.” The male stood back, holding the door open wide, and Niniane would have raced into the house, except Xanthe grabbed her arm and stopped her.

"You and you," Xanthe said, pointing to two of the guards. "Come inside with us. The rest of you, check the perimeter of the house. Guard all exit points, doors and windows." She released Niniane's arm and ran into the house with her, followed by the two guards.

The interior was a blur of rich wood furniture and golden, glowing lamps. Riordan's major domo led them up the stairs to where several servants stood, weeping. Xanthe's stomach was tight with raw nerves. She and Niniane looked through the open doors of an apartment.

Inside was an expansive, elegantly masculine bedroom, the hangings to a large bed pulled back. Two people, a male and a female, were working over a lax, bloody body. Power surged and eddied around the three of them. Xanthe clenched her teeth as nausea welled her body rebelling at the sight. As quickly as it hit, it passed, leaving a sheen of cold sweat on her hands and face.

"If you've come to gawk, get out," said the male without looking up. "I won't have his lordship subjected to it."

"I'm not here to gawk," Niniane said shortly.

The man's head jerked around. "Your Majesty—my profound apologies—"

"Forget about it. Focus on your patient. Is he—will he—?" Niniane's voice stopped abruptly as she clenched a fist in Xanthe's uniform sleeve.

The physician turned back to his patient. He said tersely, "I don't know. With respect, please leave us to work now."

"Yes, of course," Niniane whispered.

Xanthe put an arm around the smaller woman's shoulders, hugging Niniane tightly against her side. She did not know if she did so for Niniane or for herself. She could not look away from the man on the bed. His bare, well formed chest was mottled with sword gashes. A blackened bruise disfigured fully half of his still face, and oh gods, all that blood.

Xanthe had seen such terrible wounds before. Most of those who had suffered them had died. Riordan disappeared in a wet haze as her eyes filled. She cleared her throat and said huskily, "Come, let's find a sitting room."

"Of course," Niniane whispered again.

Riordan's major domo had just shown them to a sitting room when Tiago blazed into the house. It took some effort to endure the Wyr lord's presence when he was in a rage. Xanthe retreated as Tiago enfolded Niniane in his arms and asked her questions filled with quiet urgency.

Xanthe stepped out into the hall and looked for the major domo. When she found him, she asked, "How did it happen?"

He looked at her with red rimmed eyes. "We don't know, ma'am. The Chancellor was late. Well, he almost always works late these days. Tonight he was later than usual. He always tells us, you see, whenever he has an engagement or is detained. He's a thoughtful lord, a good lord."

"I know he is," she whispered.

"But he didn't come, and he didn't send word. Finally I sent two servants to look for him. They found him in the park like this. It was clear he had fought. There was blood everywhere. I sent for the physicians then to the palace."

Rage whipped through Xanthe, its sting as harsh as a cat-o-nine tail. "Why did he not have guards with him?"

The major domo blinked rapidly. "It was not his way. He said it was such a short walk from the palace grounds to his doorstep, he felt stupid calling for a guard every time he made the journey."

She pulled herself up short. The major domo did not deserve her rage. The people who attacked Riordan did. She nodded to him and left him with a quiet word of thanks, returning to wait with Niniane and Tiago in the sitting room. They didn't seem to mind when she reappeared, but she went to the window anyway and pretended to stand guard there.

The dark hours trickled by and turned to the bleak gray before dawn when the major domo stepped into the open doorway. "The physicians ask that you come," he said.

Niniane and Tiago rushed out of the room and raced up the stairs, with Xanthe close behind. She followed them into the bedroom and closed the door behind her on the anxious faces awaiting in the hall. Her hands shook. Any moment now, she thought, I will be sent out to wait with the others.

But no one seemed to notice or care that she was in the room. The physicians didn't know who she was, and Tiago and Niniane paid no attention to what she did. They were both focused on the man and woman who were tiredly washing up at basins that had been placed on a nearby sideboard.

"He'll live," the woman told them. "But he almost didn't. I was certain a couple of times that his spirit had left his body." She looked at them. "His injuries were severe and extensive, and we did the best we could but there's only so much we can do. It may take several hours to a day for him to regain consciousness, and he'll need to convalesce in peace and quiet. No work and no stress, not for a few sevendays at the very least. He's a strong man, and he used a lot of that to survive. Now he'll need to rebuild that strength."

Xanthe did not truly hear anything past the first two words. As both Tiago and Niniane asked questions and the doctors answered, she slipped like a ghost around all of them and approached the unconscious man on the bed.

She was an expert at murder, and this was how murder was done—by gaining the trust of the people around the intended victim so that you become commonplace, a fact of life like an armchair or a side table. Then no one questioned you when you came close. No one saw as you slipped the stiletto between the ribs, or dropped the poison in the drink.

Or attacked a man in a small neighborhood park

She looked down at the noble face of the man who lay so quietly, his black hair spread on the pillow. He did not look peaceful. He looked worn and deeply ill, his closed eyes bruised with dark shadows. The coverlet had been pulled up to his bare shoulders. Sometimes when the injuries were so severe, a physician simply had to stop healing because an abused body could only take so much Power coursing through it. This must have been the case with Riordan, for she could see the uneven bump of bandages underneath the covering.

No one was watching, and it was, after all, such a simple thing she needed to do. She reached out a hand and touched his temple, feeling the pulse of life underneath the pads of her fingers. Then, tenderly, she stroked the silken black hair from his forehead. It was the most audacious thing she had ever done, stealing this one moment.

Some extra sense made her turn her head. Niniane stood a few feet away, staring at her. The Queen's gaze was very wide and startled, and far too perceptive. Xanthe snatched her hand back and cleared her throat. Turned away. Turned back again. She was in an agony of embarrassment.

Niniane stopped her by simply putting a hand on her arm.

Meanwhile, Tiago saw the doctors out the door and closed it firmly on everybody else again. He turned back to join Niniane and Xanthe, looking down at Riordan

"We'll have to investigate everybody," he said. "That includes everyone in his household, of course, and his staff at the palace. The neighbors will need to be canvassed."

"I know who did this," Niniane said through set teeth.

"You think you know who instigated this," Tiago corrected as he slanted a dark look at her. "It could have actually been carried out by almost anybody."

Xanthe said, "We came through the park where his servants found him. It is a small neighborhood space, with a few trees and benches, and a little shrubbery around the edges. There is almost no place to hide. If someone lay in wait for him there, they would have looked out of place. And there would have been the sounds of the attack. No one heard or came to help him, so it is likely the inhabitants of the neighboring houses were out at some function. His attackers probably watched and waited for just such a time."

Tiago and Niniane both regarded her with thoughtful, set expressions. "There were any number of dinners and parties this evening," Niniane said.

"I'll track down who received which invitations, and which ones they attended," Tiago said.

"Sir, your grace, please give me leave to investigate this," Xanthe said between her teeth.

"No," Tiago said. "This hunt is mine." He looked at down Niniane as he rubbed her back. "He cannot remain here while I investigate. We will need to move him to the palace where we can guarantee his safety, at least until I clear his servants."

Niniane remained focused so intently on Xanthe, she had to control the urge to twitch. It was impossible to tell what the Queen was thinking. Would she say anything about Xanthe's inappropriate behavior? Perhaps Niniane might even dismiss her. Xanthe braced herself.

Niniane said to her, "You have a cottage, about an hour's walk outside the city."

Whatever she expected, it hadn't been this. She blinked, and said, "Yes, your grace."

"It is quiet there? Away from major traffic of any kind?" When she nodded, Niniane looked up at Tiago. "What about neighbors?"

He tilted his head, considering her. "I got a good look at the land when I flew out there. There aren't any neighbors in sight of the cottage. The nearest one is a farm some distance away."

"I think we should take Aubrey there," Niniane said. "The cottage is quiet and out of the way. Until you finish investigating his palace staff and his household servants, the cottage would be the safest place for him. Xanthe can tend to him and guard him, and nobody will ever think to look for him there."

Astonishment held Xanthe so frozen she didn't blink, or breathe.

Tiago murmured to Niniane, "There you go again, not following a logical path from A to B then C. You always leap to some part of the alphabet that's a complete surprise to me, and yet it makes perfect sense."

A ghost of a sparkle came into the Queen's exhausted gaze. She asked, "It's a good idea, isn't it?"

"It's an excellent idea. I can take him to the roof, change and fly him there. I'll cloak myself so that nobody will know. He'll just vanish into thin air." He looked at Xanthe. "You will do it, won't you—guard him until we have found those responsible for this?"

Xanthe's hands shook as she turned to stare at Riordan's still face. He would be in her home, where almost no one ever came. He would convalesce in her bed. She could make certain that he was safe.

"Oh, my lord," she whispered. "Yes."

Chapter Four

The Depths

HE WOKE.

Pain and exhaustion pinned him. He lay in a strange bed, in a strange room. The day was unusually quiet. There were no sounds of carriages or distant voices, just the occasional call from birds. Sunshine slanted in through a partially shaded, open window. Wind wafted gently into the room. There was a doorway to another room, where another open doorway showed flagstones and the edge of green grass.

Strange covers were drawn up over his chest and arms. They bore down heavily on him. He tried to move and couldn't, and while he was trying, he fell asleep.

When he woke again, daylight had almost faded completely. It was much cooler and the room was filled with deep shadows. He recognized nothing about the scene except for the pain he was in. His bones ached, a deep insistent throb, and he was still exhausted.

An echo of clashing swords drifted through his memory. Probably someone had kidnapped him. He found it hard to care at the moment, except if he was not dead, the whole event would turn into another long, dreary saga.

He closed his eyes and drifted.

The memory of the swordfight came back, stronger and clearer. The park, late at night. A triad of attackers. He fought hard, and he might have had a chance except for that first crippling blow that struck him from behind.

If he hadn't sensed something and started to turn, the blow would have killed him. As it was, it cut through several major muscles in his back. Still he had tried, putting viciousness into every thrust and parry, while his defeat flowed down over the back of his legs in a hot red tide and he knew he was going to die, and really, in some ways, the realization was a relief.

A quiet noise broke through the memory. Someone moved around in the other room, and his eyes flared open again. Of course he wasn't alone.

A slim straight figure appeared in the doorway then stepped into the room. The waning light fell on the familiar features of the Queen's new attendant, Xanthe Tenanye.

Bitter disappointment lanced through him, and a sickeningly familiar sense of betrayal. He said savagely, "Better me than the Queen, I suppose, or have you taken her too?"

A smile had begun to spread over her face, and something had lightened her gaze. She froze, both smile and light dying. Expressionless and calm, she said with exquisite politeness, "You have been unconscious since the attack last night. I will need to check your bandages soon, my lord, but that can wait until the morning. There is broth and bread. You may not yet feel ready to eat, but it would be good if you could drink some broth. You almost d—you lost a lot of fluid."

Almost died. Yes, that sounded about right.

He fixed his gaze on the ceiling's rafters. Since he was not really suicidal, and he had not died, he supposed he'd better take in some sustenance. He would need strength for the upcoming ordeal. He bit out, "Very well."

She seemed to hesitate. Then out of the corner of his eye, he saw her bow her head and leave the room.

Why had she started to smile? That look in her eyes. She looked like he had kicked her in the teeth before that perfect, polite wall of hers had come down.

Come to think of it, why was he bandaged?

His assailants had not fought to overcome him. They had fought to kill him.

Realization stung him. He said, "Xanthe."

He could not put much strength into his voice, but she heard him anyway and appeared again in the doorway of the bedroom. This time she remained in shadow, and he could not see her face, although he knew what she would look like. Perfect, expressionless.

"I am an old fool who has let himself become ruled by bitterness and disappointment," he said tiredly. His meager strength was waning fast again. "I apologize for the conclusion I leapt to so erroneously. You did not deserve that."

She moved forward quickly, coming into the light, and there was expression back in her face, shimmering in her eyes. "Please do not distress yourself, my lord. You have been badly injured, and you awakened to find yourself in a strange place with no explanation."

He closed his eyes. "Yes."

Gentle fingers touched his forehead then his cheek. Checking for fever, he supposed. Her hand felt warm, so he doubted he had one.

"Where am I?" he whispered. Speaking out loud was too hard to continue.

"You are at my cottage," Xanthe said softly. Her quiet, calm demeanor was soothing. "Her grace and Tiago decided you should be brought completely outside of Adriyel, while they searched for who did this to you. Tiago brought you here in secret. Except for the Queen, Tiago and I, no one knows where you are. You are safe."

He should never have doubted this straight, shining woman's dedication. The damn covers still felt as heavy as a ton of bricks, prohibiting gesture. He felt the urge to turn his face to her warm, gentle hand, and a scant moment later, he was shocked to realize he had. "Thank you."

She cupped his cheek. "I am so—glad that I could somehow be of service to you."

"What do we know?" Inevitably his thoughts turned to the Ealduns. Had they discovered that Sebrin was digging into the case they had built against him? They wouldn't have been goaded to violence by the threat of any of that becoming known, would they? After all, it would have come to light anyway had the lawsuit been allowed to continue.

He hadn't heard from the junior secretary since the other man had left Adriyel for the Ealduns' family holdings, but then he hadn't expected to, as it was a journey of some days away. Was Sebrin all right?

Xanthe did not bother to ask him what he meant. She said, "Nothing yet. We transported you as soon as the physicians had finished working on you. Tiago will return in a few days with more supplies. We can hope to learn something then. I'll fetch the broth and bread."

"Do not trouble yourself," he mumbled around the cotton that seemed to have filled his mouth. "I'm afraid it will have to wait until morning."

"Then rest well, my lord."

She sounded far away. Any further thought or speculation disappeared into cool evening shadow.

OVER THE NEXT three days, he slept, and woke, and slept again, until he could not tell if his body ached from the healing wounds or from being confined so long to bed. When he was awake, he lay watching the line of sunlight from the nearby window move along the corner of the quilt, his mind a tired blank. If he made any noise at all, and quite often even when he didn't, Xanthe was there, patiently spooning broth or water between his lips.

She changed his bandages a few times, and it was such an utter misery he had to bite his lip to keep from moaning.

On the morning of the fourth day, birdsong woke him early. He moved unguardedly and swore. Suddenly Xanthe was leaning over him, her dark gaze concerned. "It's all right," he said. "I just forgot." His mouth and throat were a burning desert. "I need a drink, please."

"Of course. I have some water here." She turned away and back to him, holding a cup. "I'm going to lift up your head up."

They had established a routine. He nodded. She slid an arm under his shoulders, bracing him as she lifted gently and held the cup to his mouth. He drank slowly, savoring the cool liquid sliding down his throat. She cradled him against her breast. When he had finished drinking all that he wanted, he leaned his head against her, savoring the warm contact with her body even more than he had the liquid.

If artifice had a scent, to him it smelled like Naida's perfumes. He had thrown out everything in her bedroom and had it scrubbed from ceiling to floor, yet now and then he still swore that he caught a whiff of her musky perfume. It made him nauseous.

Xanthe smelled nothing of artifice. She had a clean, simple scent, like sunshine and soap.

She asked, "Any more?"

He felt the small vibration of her voice against his temple and cheek. Reluctantly, he said, "No, thank you."

She eased him back onto his pillows. She looked serious, intent. "I should check your bandages again."

"Certainly," he said, bracing himself.

He had to give her credit. She made the unpleasant task as painless as possible. Her perfect expressionless face was back, insisting there was an invisible wall between them as her gentle hands unwound bandages and she checked the wounds.

He looked down at his bare body dispassionately as she worked. He had no embarrassment over his nudity, and he supposed he was made well enough, but the long gashes were red and ugly, and the wound to his back ached and throbbed insistently. He would have to take care not to tear open the knitting muscle.

"This is good," she murmured. "I think we can leave them off now."

"Hoopla," he said. He gave her a one-sided smile. "I actually mean that."

She grinned. "Do you want some more broth?"

"Gods, no," he said, and she laughed. He told her with surprise, "I'm really hungry."

"Excellent. I found some quail eggs yesterday evening. I will bring you some breakfast in a little bit."

She gathered up the bandages and left the room, returning shortly with scrambled eggs and pan biscuits that had been toasted to a golden brown. She settled into a sitting position on the bed beside him. "My apologies for the simple fare. Tiago will be coming some time day, which is a good thing, since our food supply has dwindled. We've got tea, oil and dry oats. If he's detained for any reason, I will have to do a bit of foraging and hunting."

"This is wonderful," he said in all truthfulness. The steaming eggs were golden and the pan biscuits were delicious. He ate all of the eggs and a biscuit, and then with the abruptness of a convalescent tumbled headlong into sleep.

The sound of voices woke him. Tiago and Niniane were talking with Xanthe in the next room. "This is a wonderful place," Niniane said.

"It is very small," Xanthe said. "My father built it for us after my mother died."

"Your father was a true craftsman. It's beautifully done. The furniture is lovely, and so is the floor."

Aubrey glanced over the edge of the bed at the planed hardwood floors that bore the smooth patina of age. "We brought half the marketplace with us," Tiago said.

"And this bag is full of books," said Niniane. "This one is full of clothes for Aubrey. And this one is full of games. You have plenty here with which to occupy yourselves, as soon as Aubrey is feeling up to it."

"We certainly do," said Xanthe. "This is all so much more than I expected."

Niniane said, "We wanted to make sure you had everything you needed, in case we were unable to return right away."

Xanthe asked quickly, "There are problems?"

"There are complications," Tiago said, stressing the last word. "None of it is anything we can't handle, but we are busy. And Niniane and I have both agreed that no one else is to know that Aubrey is here. You will be on your own until we can return again."

"Yes, sir."

Aubrey clenched his fists and contemplated getting out of bed. He felt immensely better than he had even earlier that morning, and he could tell that he had turned a corner. He eased himself to a sitting position awkwardly. Any unwary movement made his back flare with fiery pain. Breathing deeply, he eased his legs over the edge of the bed.

"How is Aubrey?" Niniane asked.

Aubrey said hoarsely, "I'm awake."

He listened to a symphony of footsteps, one quick, light patter, another light step with a longer stride, and a deeper, heavier tread. He checked to make sure that the sheet was wrapped around his hips as Niniane burst into the bedroom. She threw herself at him, pulling up just before she made contact to put her arms carefully around him.

"I cannot tell you how scared I was for you," she whispered.

He hugged her as he looked over her head at Tiago and at Xanthe. He said gently, "The scare is all over with now." He met Tiago's black gaze. "What has happened since the attack?"

"We are not here to discuss details of the

investigation," Tiago said. "Your assailants will not get away unpunished. That's all you need to know, until we come back for you and tell you that you can return home."

Aubrey's face hardened. He opened his mouth to argue, and Niniane put a hand to his cheek, turning him to look at her. Her face was sober, eyes still moist. "Aubrey, you nearly died."

"I know that," he snapped.

"Then listen to me, because I am very serious and I mean every word," Niniane told him. "Your job is to get better. Rest, eat good food, soak up sunshine and heal. That's all. You cannot work. You will not leave this place. This is your safe haven for now. Tiago will return with more food in a week. In the meantime, we will not stop until we have in custody everyone who is responsible for what happened to you. You will be able to come home soon enough, and then you'll have your answers."

He gritted his teeth as rage coursed through him. Not rage at Niniane, but at the people who had attacked him. It was hard to let go of it. After a moment he said, "I will stay until I am completely healed. Then I can ensure my own safety."

"No, Aubrey." The Queen's gaze was adamant. "I am ordering you to stay until I say that you can leave."

"Niniane," he said.

"Oh, I know you're mad at me now. Deal with it." She hugged him again.

He set his teeth but put an arm around her. Looking at Tiago, he said, "At least do one thing for me. I want you to check on one of my staff. His name is Sebrin. I sent him to uncover what he could about the Ealduns' lawsuit, and I hadn't heard from him since."

Tiago and Niniane shared a long, inscrutable look before Tiago promised, "I'll look into it."

Niniane stood. "I'm sorry our visit is so short, but we can't stay any longer." She looked at Xanthe. "Take care of him."

"I will," Xanthe promised.

She trailed behind Niniane and Tiago who left. Aubrey breathed evenly as he glared at the open window. He listened to their voices fade as they moved away from the cottage. If he thought he could stand without falling, he would have followed them to argue.

After a few minutes Xanthe returned. She moved around in the other room then appeared in his doorway carrying two large canvas bags on her shoulders. He glowered at her, which was a totally useless display of petulance as she did not look at him directly. She wore her perfect expressionless face again.

He had been amused by that smooth façade of hers before, but now it was beginning to grate on him. Silence reigned in the room as she opened first one bag and pulled out a pile of folded clothes and boots. She set them on the bed beside him then opened the other bag and pulled out twenty books. Some of them were American paperbacks, and a few were Dark Fae. He glanced at the titles as she stacked them neatly on the small, simple bedside table. None of the books were nonfiction.

Xanthe returned to the pile of clothes on the bed and broke the silence. "Would you like a pair of trousers and a shirt?"

His hand shot out to circle her wrist. She stilled and looked down at his hand. "As soon as I am better, you will take me back to Adriyel."

Her dark gaze lifted to meet his. "No, my lord."

He said, his voice edged, "I did not ask you. I ordered you to."

One of her silken eyebrows raised, a small quirk of reaction. "You may issue as many orders as you like, but I am not obligated to obey you," she said. "I am not your servant. I am the Queen's. You may be willing to defy her orders, but I will not disrespect or disobey her."

There was that loyalty of hers, straight and unwavering. He thought back to his disappointed sense of betrayal when he had so briefly thought she had kidnapped him, and his unruly temper subsided.

He remarked in a much milder tone, "I'm acting like an ass, aren't I?"

Her demeanor softened. "You're angry, and understandably so. It's hard to have your movements restricted, especially when you feel the need to act."

"This has happened to you too," he said. "You must stay here with me."

One corner of her mouth lifted. "Truly, it is not a

hardship. I want to do it. But before her grace came up with this idea, I had asked to be the one to hunt for your attackers. Tiago denied me, and it was very hard. He's hunting for all those responsible, himself."

She had wanted to hunt down those who attacked him? He blinked, and his grip loosened.

The last several days had given him a deep, visceral knowledge of her, the timbre of her voice, her scent, the gentle touch of her hands on his body. Following an impulse to learn more about her by touch, he let his fingers slide over her forearm as he slowly let go of her. The texture of her skin was silken, warm.

She took in a quick, near silent breath. As he stared into her eyes he saw her pupils dilate.

She reacted to his touch.

What was he doing? He frowned and released her fully.

She angled her face away as she gathered up the pile of clothes. "Please leave trousers and a shirt," he said.

She nodded and did so, then took the rest of the clothes to set them on the nearby dresser. Afterward, she turned to him, not quite looking at him. "Do you require assistance with dressing?"

He hesitated as he struggled with his pride. It wasn't just his rage; all his emotions were unruly. Normally even tempered, he felt like a stranger to himself. At last, he admitted, "I don't know."

She glanced at his face quickly and nodded. "Call if you have need."

"Thank you."

She stepped out of the room, and he shook out the trousers. Those he could manage, one leg at a time, although his muscles shook when he stood upright to pull them over his hips. The shirt was something else entirely. He could slide one arm into a sleeve, but could not flex his back muscles enough to fully don it.

Instead of calling out to her, he stood again, forcing his knees to lock and accept his full weight. Then he walked carefully across the room, his bare feet making no sound on the smooth floorboards. When he reached the doorway, he leaned one shoulder against its support and looked curiously around the other room.

It was more spacious than the bedroom, with a large kitchen cupboard and shelves along one wall, a table and two chairs, and two more armchairs positioned in front of the fireplace. There was a sideboard with a basin and bucket for washing dishes and preparing meals. A sheathed sword in a shoulder harness hung on a simple hook beside the doorway that stood open to the sunny morning.

All of the furniture was made of plain, solid oak that had been polished to a warm golden color. The armchairs had seat cushions that looked worn and comfortable. As with many Dark Fae country cottages, the large fireplace was the heart of the house, a true cooking fireplace with walk-in room and a swiveling iron bar from which hung a cooking pot.

Beside the fireplace was a shadowed alcove with a

curtain pushed open. He could see the edge of a copper tub. There was also a simple pallet on the floor. He paused at that thoughtfully, looking back into 'his' room. There was only one bed in the cottage, and he was using it.

Xanthe was busy unpacking two more large canvas bags. She looked at each package, container or jar interestedly, muttering to herself as she set the items on the table, which was already piled high with fresh fruits and vegetables.

He opened his mouth to ask for her help but then hesitated. Instead, obeying again some nameless impulse, he tilted his head and watched her work. She had a quiet, peaceful demeanor, and she looked comfortable, at home with her own company. For the first time, he realized that she wasn't dressed in a palace black uniform, but instead wore a soft looking, somewhat worn tunic and trousers. Her hair was braided, but not as tightly as usual, and the dark length shone with auburn highlights in the slice of sunlight that fell across her back and shoulders.

His gaze lingered on the gentle curve of her cheek then dropped to the swell of her breasts, where he had rested his head earlier. Her hips were slight and trim but definitely feminine. She was not as tall as he, but her legs were lean and long.

She looked up toward the doorway, saw that he was watching her, and a delicate tinge of color washed over her face. She glanced at his shirt that hung off one shoulder and set aside a wax wheel of cheese to walk over to him quickly.

"You should have said something," she said.

He raised his eyebrows. "Did you just scold me?"

She jerked to a halt, the color in her cheeks deepening. "I—I'm sorry, my lord."

She looked so flustered, he found himself smiling. He asked gently, "Xanthe, would you mind helping me slip into this blasted shirt?"

Her gaze flew up to his, to his bare shoulders and chest, and darted away. "Not at all," she said. She sounded winded.

He could barely stand on his feet, and his body still throbbed with pain. But something else stirred, something that had been buried under grief and anger and had lain dormant for a long while.

She came closer to carefully ease him fully into the shirt, and his back muscles protested only a small bit as she supported the full weight of his arm.

He was taller than she was by half a head. He bent his head close to hers, inhaling her fresh, clean scent. "Thank you."

She tilted her head slightly, so that they stood almost cheek to cheek. If she raised her head a little more, if he lowered his....

"You're welcome," she whispered.

This was too intimate. He straightened. "I see Tiago was not joking when he said they brought half the marketplace."

She widened her gaze. "There are even biscuits and a pot of clotted cream. I haven't reached the bottom of the bags yet. If I fish for supper occasionally and forage for sun potatoes and fresh greens, we have enough food for weeks." She paused then asked hesitantly, "Would you like to sit at the table while I put things away?"

For a moment he was tempted but another wave of dizziness washed over him. He gritted his teeth, hating his own weakness. "Perhaps later," he said. "Right now, I think I need to lie down again."

"Of course." She stepped close, put her arm around his waist and helped him back to the bed.

Darkness danced around the edge of his vision. He muttered, "I've taken your only bed and put you on the floor."

"That does not matter."

He eased back onto the pillows. "It matters to me."

The darkness grew closer, hazing his mind. As if from a great distance, he felt her tuck the sheet over him. He thought he heard her say, "That is why people care about you so much."

Then his unruly emotions and wayward mind grew quiet, as the darkness took him over completely.

Chapter Five

The Dance

XANTHE TOOK THE perishables like the eggs and clotted cream, loaded them carefully into the wire well basket, and then lowered them into the cool deep water of the well. She kept a few of the eggs out to boil them. While those cooked, she found storage places for rest of the food.

There were also biscuits, fresh bread, jams and jellies, cheese, both fresh and salted meat, nuts, three kinds of tea, butter, flour, barley, sugar, fruits and vegetables. Sweet potatoes. There were even three bars of soap that smelled like honeyed almonds and were rich enough that fine ladies would not distain using them. This cottage had never seen such rich fare.

Xanthe was no fancy cook, but she could prepare good, plain meals, and all the luxuries from the market would help to dress up anything she might offer. By the time Aubrey awakened again, she had a substantial lunch prepared of the last of the chicken, sautéed turnip greens, boiled eggs, and bread, butter and jam. In small bowls were fresh berries sprinkled with sugar.

She was just about to retrieve the clotted cream from the well when she heard his quiet footsteps. She turned as he entered the room. He ran his hands through loose raven hair. His clothes were rumpled, and his feet were still bare. It was shocking to see him in any way less than meticulously groomed and in formal clothing. As she studied his stance and angular features, she was pleased to see that he was much steadier already.

He said, "I see that you have been busy."

"Are you hungry?"

His gaze lit upon the contents on the table. "I am."

She had not been sure how to lay out the meal, if he might need to stay in bed or if he would rather she did not eat with him. But this was, after all, her home. There was only one place to sit and eat, and also, he had not seemed to mind in the slightest when she had joined him and Tiago for breakfast, so she had laid two settings.

His gait was steady, if a bit stiff, as he walked over to ease into one of the chairs. The reality of sitting across from him and eating alone with him started to sink in.

She remembered the clotted cream and said awkwardly, "I almost forgot something—I'll be right back."

He snagged hold of her hand when she would have walked away. Her insides churned at the warm grasp. Although she would have given anything for him not to have been so badly wounded, already there were so many moments of this experience that she would hold close and treasure afterward. Chief among them was every time he touched her.

He looked up at her. The gold of the sun glimmered in his light gray eyes. "Thank you for this, Xanthe. Thank you for everything."

She turned her hand to clasp his and press briefly at his lean fingers, as she said, entirely truthfully, "It is truly my pleasure, my lord."

"I expect you to start calling me Aubrey," he said as he returned the squeeze of her fingers and released her. "After all, as you so eloquently pointed out, you are not my servant."

He was nobility, while she was a commoner. She forced her lips to move. "That would not be appropriate."

He winked at her. "As Tiago would say, screw appropriate."

Winked. At her.

She should probably respond in some manner to what he had said, but her mind seized up, so she gave up and fled the cottage.

When she drew up the wire basket from the well to retrieve the pot of cream, she splashed cold water on her face and stood for a moment with her head bent, the water dripping from her nose and chin.

"Aubrey," she whispered. The sweet pain, that honeyed stiletto, pierced her all over again.

When she returned indoors, he was watching the dying flames in the cookfire, his food untouched. He had waited for her. That embarrassed her for some reason. She opened the pot and set it on the table as she slipped into her seat. She muttered, "For the berries."

Aubrey picked up his knife and fork. "Niniane knows I have a sweet tooth. It was kind of her to indulge it."

"We have steak for this evening," she told him. "And a roast for tomorrow. After that, it will be fish and salt meat. If you like, I can use the roast for a field stew." A field stew was traditional hunter's fare and often combined sweet and savory flavors.

"I love field stew. It's the only thing I know how to cook, although it has been some time since I have actually hunted." He gave her another smile to add to her treasure of memories. "Niniane was right, this cottage is charming. Your father did a wonderful job."

"Thank you." She looked around as if seeing it through fresh eyes. To someone of Aubrey's stature and wealth, it must seem like a very humble place.

"Where is your father now?"

The bite she had taken turned to dust in her mouth. She forced herself to swallow. "He was one of the palace guards who died the night Urien seized power."

Aubrey paused eating as well. "I'm very sorry."

"It was a long time ago." She gave him a quick smile. "I was only a new recruit in the army, so I was nowhere near the palace that night."

He studied her. "You stayed a soldier despite what had happened?"

Her shoulders stiffened. "I did. I worked hard and eventually became a palace guard. I had a dream of one day taking Urien completely by surprise and sinking my knife into his back. The chance never came. When Tiago employed me, I told that to him in the interview. He liked that I could be so patient while I looked for an opportunity. He called the last two hundred years my hunting season." She lifted her gaze to Aubrey's face. Would he be repulsed by what she had just confessed?

He didn't look in the least repulsed. His expression was open and accepting. As they finished the main portion of their meal, he took the pot of cream, spooning some onto her berries first before he helped himself. The small courtesy warmed her.

He said, "After Urien killed Rhian and Shaylee who were my friends, the hardest thing I ever did was to remain Chancellor when he renewed my appointment. In fact, several of my other friends could not accept it and they cut me off. A few have begun speaking to me again, but I no longer care for their regard."

She said, "You hated Urien too."

"Of course I did," he said. His face had turned hard, the angles of the graceful bones standing out against his pale skin. "Passionately. It kept me awake at night. It poisoned the savor of my meals. But the Dark Fae and the welfare of Adriyel meant more to me than my own rancor. I tempered Urien's actions whenever I possibly could, went behind his back when I thought I could get away with it, and did everything in my power to help steer the congress and the courts on a steady path."

Xanthe set aside her spoon. She said carefully, "I respect Niniane as my Queen, and in a very short time, I have grown to love her, so please do not mistake what I say. What you did has not gone unrecognized. I, along with everybody that I know, hoped that you would be crowned king. Those so-called friends of yours—while their first reaction was understandable, to go all that time without speaking to you was exceedingly short sighted, judgmental and cruel."

The hardness eased gradually from his face as he listened. He gave her a faint smile that was little more than a crinkling of his eyes at the edges. "Thank you." He scraped the bottom of his bowl. "This was a delicious meal, and the company was even more delightful. I absolutely refuse to fall asleep again."

She laughed. "Sleep is your body's way of recovering, but if you would rather, we can spread a blanket for you under a tree while you explore the pile of books Niniane and Tiago left."

"That sounds perfect." He watched while she cleared the table and stacked the dishes in the basin. Then he held his side with a wince as he yawned widely.

She suspected his fight against sleep would not last long. Not only had his injuries taxed his resources, so had the healing. The physician had ordered at least two sevendays of convalescence for a reason.

She took a blanket outside for him and shook it out in the shade of a large elm tree that was located near the front door. He appeared a few moments later, carrying three books, and struggled to kneel on the blanket. She hovered beside him, anxious to help, but his savage expression held her back.

When he was seated on the ground, he eased himself back until he was prone. She went into the cottage and returned with a pillow.

"Thank you," he said. The skin around his mouth was white.

"You're welcome." She watched for a moment as he selected one of the books and began to read. Then she went to draw water to clean the dishes.

When she was finished, she looked outside. His eyes were closed, his book resting on his chest. She grinned. Each time he fell asleep he woke up stronger. This time, he might even wake up grumpier.

After she had washed and put away the dishes, she puttered around for a bit. She made the bed and boiled the bandages that he had worn. When they were thoroughly cleansed, she hung them in the sun. After they dried, she would roll and store them.

The rest of the cottage was already tidy. There was more than enough food. In a few days, she would have to do laundry, but for now there wasn't anything that required attention until it was time to cook supper.

An invisible leash pulled her to the sleeping man underneath the shade tree. Silently she eased herself down to sit on one corner of the blanket. She felt as guilty as if she were stealing, but she couldn't help herself. Studying him at leisure without fear of discovery was an almost unimaginable luxury.

He did not look quite so desperately ill, but he still looked worn. Shadows under his eyes lingered, as did the brackets of pain around his mouth. Tenderness pulled at her.

It was one thing to admire him from a distance for all the fine things he embodied. It was totally different to grow to know him a little, and to see the real man behind the reputation. He struggled with his temper, chafed at illness and injury, carried shadows of loneliness in those kind eyes.

Instead of showing her that her idol had feet of clay, all these things served to highlight just how outstanding his long service to his country had been. How many times had he felt endangered by Urien? Probably too often to count. When he had lain awake at night, did he, too, wonder if he might die friendless and alone?

If he had cared at all about his wife—and she believed that he had for he was a caring man—he had no doubt relied upon her companionship and drew comfort from her support, which would have made the crimes that she had committed doubly terrible for him.

She watched him quietly as the sun traveled through the sky and the dappled shade moved across his long, relaxed body. When he began to stir, she shot to her feet and fled into the house. She had her weapons laid out on the table and her sword drawn and was busy polishing and sharpening blades when Aubrey's shadow fell into the room. She kept her head tucked down, gaze focused on her task.

He said nothing as he stood and watched her. The moment spun on an enchanted spindle until it drew out, long and golden like a thread of dyed flax pulling taut between them. She would not look up. She could not. She did not feel in control of herself, and she was terrified at what might show in her eyes.

Finally he moved quietly into the bedroom.

Her fingers shook. She nicked one on the blade she had just sharpened. She sucked the injured finger and thought, I am a fool.

When she finished with her task, she sheathed all her weapons and hung them in their customary spot beside the cottage door. Somehow the day had fled so that it was time to cook supper. She had set sweet potatoes to bake in the coals of the lunch cook fire, so all that she needed to do was grill the steaks and prepare a fresh salad of mixed greens and vegetables.

She stepped outside to collect an armful of wood. When she came back into the cottage, Aubrey appeared. He was still barefoot, and he had unbuttoned his shirt. It hung open on his wide shoulders. The wounds on his long, lean torso were already fading. This time when Aubrey raised his hands to his loose hair, he worked with a wince to tie the length back with a leather strip. It caused his chest muscles to bunch and flow under his skin.

She looked at the rippling hollows of his flat

abdomen where his muscles were tightened, and her breath grew restricted. She had to force enough air into lungs to tell him, "Once the fire is ready, supper won't be long."

He wore a tense, sour expression. "I dislike watching you fix meals and fuss."

She stared down at the wood she carried, blinking. "Have I fussed? I am sorry. But we must eat."

He moved abruptly. "That is not what I meant. I'm the one who is sorry. You have not fussed. You've done nothing but show me patience and kindness, even when I'm sure I've been tactless and did not deserve it. I am frustrated that you are doing all the work. I dislike watching you labor while I do nothing." He gave a sharp sigh. "I am unused to doing nothing."

That she could understand. She was unused to doing nothing as well. She looked at him sideways and gave him a sly smile. "It sounds as though you are beginning to feel better."

He chuckled. "I must be, since my temper has turned so foul. What can I do to help?"

Shocked, her gaze flew wide. "Nothing!"

He advanced on her with a determined expression, and she backed up until her shoulders hit the wall behind her. "I do not accept that answer."

"You are the one who was severely injured. I am perfectly healthy, and it is my job to look after you and do the work." She hugged the armful of wood as he tried to take the top few logs. "Stop that! You're still healing, and you might strain one of those wounds."

"I am well aware of what my body can and cannot do, thank you." He tugged and she pulled back, until he pointed out in a plaintive voice, "You know this tug of war can't be good for me."

She stared at him in wounded astonishment. Oh, that was playing entirely naughty. She stopped instantly, her hold loosening. As he took the top logs from her armload, she glared at him, mouth folded tight in disapproval.

He paused, and one corner of his mouth tilted up as he studied her. "You should see what you look like right now," he told her.

"I have no idea what you're talking about," she muttered as she hitched her remaining armload up higher.

He folded his mouth tight and glared at her.

Completely off kilter, she stared, and her own mouth dropped open. "I don't look that bad!"

"No," he agreed, the expression vanishing. "You are much prettier than me."

"Don't be ridiculous!" She scuttled sideways to get around him then rushed to the fireplace to throw her armload onto the hearth. It scattered wood debris everywhere, and the floor would have to be swept again. She didn't care. Then her next thought just fell out of her mouth. "You're the most handsome man I know."

The instant the words left her lips, she would have snatched them out of the air if she could. Her face burned.

He moved up beside her and squatted to ease the logs he had purloined onto the hearth with hers.

She watched with round, unblinking eyes as he straightened and turned to face her.

He thinks I'm pretty?

He was smiling, and it looked satisfied and very male. "So you think I'm handsome."

She scrambled to backtrack somehow. Heaven only knew where her poise had gone. The afternoon sun must have baked it out of her head. "Of course you look—distinguished," she accused. "You know perfectly well you do."

Of all the ridiculous things to say. She was going from bad to worse. She spun on her heel, retreated to put the table between them and began pulling food items off the shelves without really looking at what she was doing.

He followed at a leisurely pace across the room, almost as if he was stalking her.

Then he came all the way around the table.

He—what was he doing?

"You didn't say distinguished before," he pointed out. "You said handsome. I remember that fact quite fondly."

"DidI-Ihadn'tnoticed," she mumbled all in a rush. She had forgotten what she was supposed to be doing. If she had ever known in the first place.

"Xanthe, are you shy?" he murmured. "I didn't know

assassins could be shy. This realization is remarkable."

"Don't be stupid, I'm never shy," she blurted. She had disrobed in front of dozens of other soldiers countless of times. She'd had sex with no more privacy than what the cover of a blanket might offer, and she had probably heard every crude joke or epithet the army had in its repertoire. "And I'm not an assassin any longer, I'm a guard."

"Semantics, my dear." His lean, angular features were lit with delight. All shadows and marks of pain had vanished. He looked like an entirely different man from the ill, unconscious man that Tiago had brought into her cottage. He glanced over all the items she had placed at random on the table. His sleek eyebrows rose. "So we are having honey, cheese, onions and tea for supper?"

"Of course not!" Her cheeks grew hotter. She scrambled for some kind excuse for her erratic behavior. "I was just going to dust off the shelves."

He picked up the jar of honey. "Were you going to do that before or after you cook?"

She threw up her hands. "You are distracting me from what I'm supposed to be doing!"

He was laughing then, his face creased with open enjoyment, eyes dancing. "Is that what I'm doing, distracting you? I thought I was teasing you."

Witnessing him in this unpredictable, playful mode was definitely much more composure-destroying than when he had winked at her. She rushed at him and snatched the jar out of his hands. "Get out of my kitchen, so I can have some hope of cooking something edible."

He pointed out, "Your kitchen is half the cottage."

She ducked her head. "You could go outside."

"I've been outside for a significant part of the day already."

"Go to bed then."

"I have spent a significant part of the day there too," he said softly. "And I feel extraordinarily guilty every time I lie in that soft bed. Inevitably I end up thinking of you, and this hard pallet on the floor that must be so very uncomfortable."

Her breathing hitched again. She picked up the cheese and turned away to start setting things back on the shelves. "I keep telling you, I don't mind in the slightest. Believe me, I have bunked down under much worse conditions many times."

"That doesn't make me feel better." He handed her the onions to set back in their place, and as she turned around again, he handed her the tin of tea. "I propose that I begin to help with the chores around here." When she opened her mouth to argue, he forestalled her. "I will only do what I feel capable of doing, and each day I will increase my activity. That will help me regain my strength much faster. I simply cannot laze my days away and watch as you shoulder the burden for doing everything. I don't have it in me."

She sighed. Increasing his activity each day would help him heal. She also knew some stretching exercises that he could do to help keep his body limber. He was going to carry scars, and those would stiffen if he wasn't careful. "That makes sense."

"And as soon as my back muscles have healed enough," he said, "you and I are going to start taking turns on that pallet."

"No, we're not," she told him.

"Yes," he said implacably. "We are."

"I won't budge on this," she warned.

His mouth quirked. "What a coincidence; neither will I."

If they grew stubborn about this, they might both end up sleeping on floor pallets. She clapped a hand over her nose and mouth as a snort of laughter escaped her.

If anyone had told her a sevenday ago that she would be arguing with a barefoot Chancellor of the Dark Fae, she would have thought them deranged. Shaking her head, she turned away from him again to set the tea tin on the shelf.

Then she sensed rather than heard him move up close behind her. She stood frozen, the skin at the back of her neck tingling as she felt the heat of his body along her back and thighs. He was very close, perhaps a scant finger's breadth away. She turned her head slightly, her attention consumed by his nearness.

She could see him, just barely, out of the corner of her eye, standing there like the shadow of her most secret dream. He tilted his head and put his lips near her ear, still not coming in physical contact with her anywhere.

He whispered, "Am I really the most handsome man you know?"

His warm breath caressed the thin, sensitive area just behind her jaw. She folded her arms around her middle, shaking. A daring stranger took over her voice. She closed her eyes and heard herself whisper back, "Do you really think I'm pretty?"

Pretty. It was a word used for Dark Fae ladies, with their fine clothes, long pale, soft hands and large, lustrous eyes. It didn't belong to her. Her hands were callused, her skin lightly speckled by the sun. Her feet were callused too. She could kill a man with a single, well placed kick of her bare foot.

The slightest touch stroked along her hair, following the line from her temple, back to her braid. Was that his finger? The end of his nose? It was so light she could almost have believed that she imagined it, yet it sent an intense shiver rippling over her skin. It was—almost as though he nuzzled her. The thought took all the strength out of her knees.

At the nape of her neck, he breathed, "I think you grow more beautiful each time I lay my eyes on you. It's happened every time I woke up to find you there, helping me in some way. All I want to do is look at you, to experience it again."

The moist warm heat of the words felt like a brand. The shiver settled low in her abdomen, and a liquid heat bloomed between her legs. Surely he would not notice if her hand trailed stealthily down her torso to press at the sharp, empty ache.

"Don't play with me just because you're bored." The words were meant to wedge some kind of distance between them and allow sanity back into the room, to cool the insane heat that built so that she could not focus for wanting to tear off all her clothes. Instead they sounded pleading.

"I would never dream of treating you in such a self-indulgent and cavalier manner." He stroked her back, another feather light touch that explored the contour of her shoulder blade and the indentation just underneath where her ribs curved to her spine. "Xanthe, I have not heard you say my name yet."

The same pleading she had heard in her own voice was in his too.

Her regard mattered to him.

Her knees weakened further, and her lips trembled.

She whispered, "Aubrey."

He was silent. She could hear him breathing. Then another brush of sensation at the back of her neck—those were his lips. He had kissed her.

"Thank you, my dear," he whispered in return as he pulled away.

Chapter Six

Sacrifice

AUBREY BACKED FROM XANTHE, his emotions more unruly than ever. Arousal coursed through his body, more powerful than the lingering aches and pains. He had grown hard, and his swollen cock, surprised into life after a year of dullness and disinterest, demanded attention most urgently.

The sensation of her soft, warm skin lingered on his lips. He licked them.

He wanted to lick her so much more.

Restlessness, irritation, his growing awareness of her as an attractive female, it had turned into an all too potent cocktail. Teasing her had been impulse. Pursuing as she retreated had been instinct. He had not thought through any of it; it had just happened, and that was unlike him as he was usually thoughtful and deliberate about everything.

His intellect wrestled with his bucking instincts. It was a tough tussle, but intellect—just barely—won.

He turned away and muttered hoarsely, "I'll start

helping by laying a fire."

"That would be nice."

Her voice shook, a telltale, vulnerable sound from such a strong, bright woman. The impulse to sexual aggression flared hot and insistent. His instincts weren't going down without a fight.

At the hearth, he forced himself to go down on one knee, and he poked at the ashes of the previous fire to see if any live embers remained. He disturbed a few charred sweet potatoes, and he rolled those over to the side then quickly laid the wood. A few glowing coals remained, and soon the fire was blazing.

He straightened from his crouch and moved to a nearby armchair to tend the fire unnecessarily. The soft sounds of movement behind him seemed as loud as a shout, proclaiming that her presence was close and vital.

He glanced over his shoulder and almost laughed. The crazy woman had put more things on the table again. This time, though, he could see that it all had a theme, fruits and vegetables, so no doubt she had meant to do it. She was chopping greens.

Her face was calm, smooth, perfectly expressionless.

Reaction roared through him. He shook with the urge to stalk over, take the knife from her hand, press her up against the wall and cover her lips with his. Spear into her mouth. Anything to strip away that façade and see what really lay underneath.

Her breathing had been unsteady. She had asked him not to toy with her. Her voice had trembled when she had whispered his name.

She had not been indifferent, gods damn it.

He rubbed his face. Maybe he really had died in the attack, and a demon of lunacy had taken over his body. This kind of impetuosity was completely outside of his normal behavior and deeply unsettling.

His wretched cock still wouldn't bend to his rule either. The air in the cottage had turned much too close and stifling. He rose to his feet and walked out.

Outside, the early evening air was much cooler. After a moment's searching, he found the covered well and drew a bucket of ice cold water.

First he drank thirstily. Then he dumped the rest of it over his head, gasping and shuddering as it cascaded all over his body. *Holy shit.* The sensation was keen as a knife, and just as painful, and a fitting way to force him to contemplate the magnitude of his own folly.

He leaned his palms on the rim of the well as water dripped off him.

The thing of it was, he couldn't remember a time before when he was ever this attracted to a woman. No doubt it had happened; he had lived a very long time, after all.

But that would have been a younger self in another time. A less tried, greener self.

It wasn't here and now, where he embodied the totality of all his experiences.

When the beauty of the spirit had come to mean so much more to him than the beauty of the body.

Where he knew a multitude of sorrows and reasons to be wary, and yet he still felt this slow burning, excruciating build-up of need.

Naida had caused him a vicious hurt precisely because he had loved her, but he had never felt anything for her that was remotely like what he was coming to feel for Xanthe. He and Naida had gone through a considered courtship, discussed together the advantages of a partnership together and had come to a mutual agreement. Everything had been very much in character, laid out, predictable.

At the time he thought it had been so very civilized, their relationship solidly grounded in friendship. Really, nothing could compare to the shock of a civilized man who came face to face with his own barbarity.

The smell of cooking steak wafted out of the cottage, and his stomach growled. His appetite for food had come back with a vengeance. It was a solid metaphor, as his appetite for other things had now resurfaced. He had sustained two serious injuries, one spiritual and the other physical, and it appeared that he would end up surviving them both after all.

As for the quiet, reserved Xanthe—he could see nothing to hold him back from going after what he now acknowledged that he wanted. He no longer had any ties or previous commitments. He was free to act on whatever he desired.

Now it was time for his own hunting season.

WHEN SHE SAW HIM step into the cottage carrying the water bucket, she rushed at him from the hearth, scolding. "You should not be carrying something that heavy so soon!"

He smiled and tilted the bucket slightly to show her the contents. "You are such a ferocious mother hen It's only half full. I said I would help and I mean to do it. I'll draw all the water for the supper dishes. It will take me twice as long, but that is quite all right as there are no urgent appointments this evening."

After glancing into the bucket, she looked up at him somewhat shamefaced. "I just don't want you to hurt yourself any further."

"I appreciate that," he said, warmed by the evidence of her caring. Deliberately, he leaned forward and pressed his lips to hers, a full, firm, yet brief caress. All too soon, he pulled away. The sensation of her lips, softened in surprise, was branded on his mouth.

She stood absolutely still, her lovely dark eyes very wide.

He would not smile. It might reveal too much triumph. He sidestepped neatly around her and went to the basin to pour water into it. Then he went outside again. By the time he returned, she had hunched over the grilling steaks and she did not look up.

He made three more trips to the well before she set the steaming steaks on the table, and he surveyed the results of his effort with satisfaction. He had drawn plenty of water for the evening dishes. Then he turned to the table. She had created a salad of greens, fresh vegetables, apples and berries, lightly dressed with oil and herbs, to accompany the steaming sweet potatoes and steak.

She also looked exceedingly spooked.

This would have to be a gentle hunt, or his prey might skedaddle.

As he took his seat at the table, he said gravely, "Thank you for another wonderful meal."

Unaccountably, she flushed as she sat as well. "I do not know how to cook the complex delicacies you are no doubt used to eating."

He kept his gaze on the contents of his plate. "Do not confuse what you imagine my lifestyle must be with what you witness at the palace. I much prefer meals like this on a daily basis." He sensed rather than saw her relax a little. They ate in silence. Now that he had turned the corner, he could almost feel the return of health and vigor with every bite of the healthy fare. As he finished, he said, "I would like to take advantage of that bathing alcove this evening, if I might."

She said quickly, "Of course. I'll draw water and put it on to heat while I do the dishes." She glanced up at him and then away, her gaze skittering off like a frightened mouse. "You will carry some scarring from those wounds. It will be good for you to soak in a hot tub with a little oil poured in the water."

He nodded. He would fetch his own bath water if he could, but he had already reached his limit. "If you would be kind enough to draw the water, I will wash the dishes—no, I do not want to hear it, Xanthe." He added that last in a stern, no nonsense voice as she began to speak. "We have already agreed upon this."

She closed her mouth with an audible click of her teeth. After a moment, she muttered, "Agreeing in theory and watching it in practice are two different things."

He said in a very gentle voice, "But you would not deny me anything that is good for me, would you?"

"Of course not," she replied in a strangled whisper, while she looked at him exasperation. He bit back a smile.

By the time he had washed the dishes and put them away, his bath water had heated to a comfortable temperature, and he soaked in the silken, lightly oiled bath until the water had cooled. Then he washed all over, luxuriating in the sensation of cleanliness.

In the pile of clothing Niniane and Tiago had brought for him was a long, warm robe, which he donned afterward. Mercifully his aches were retreating as he healed, but after supper and the light exercise, the bath had done him in.

As he pushed aside the curtain, he saw that Xanthe must have used the basin to wash as well, for her hair was wet and slicked back, and she had donned a soft dark purple shirt and trousers. Full evening had set, and the warmth from the fire mingled pleasantly with the coolness of the air that wafted in from the still open door.

She sat in one of the armchairs, looking at the fire contemplatively, which lit her profile with golden light. Desire glowed deep within him, banked in its own hearth and waiting for the right opportunity to spark into a blaze.

Something had been tickling at his awareness for some time, but he only now paid attention to it. He frowned. "There is something of Power in this room."

"Yes," she said. Her gaze flicked to the mantle. "I will show it to you, if you like."

Did she look guilty? He wondered why.

He walked over to look curiously at the items on the mantel. There was a pipe lying in a clean flat pottery dish, a beautiful piece of crystal, a small polished copper bowl and a wooden box.

"Do you smoke?" he asked, surprised. He had never smelled tobacco on her.

"No. That was my father's pipe."

Power emanated from the box. He glanced at Xanthe who hovered nearby, watching him closely. "May I?"

She took a deep breath, her fingers twisted together, and nodded.

He lifted the box up, handling it with care, and examined it from all sides before he opened it to look at the deck of cards inside. "There's a tale to tell here."

"I got it from Duncan and Seremela," she told him. "Seremela's niece had stolen it, and they didn't want to be responsible for it. I said—I said I would take care of it."

"Did you?" He turned over the first exquisitely crafted card and looked upon the fierce, golden face of Love. Then he turned over the second card to lock at the sharp, ruthless visage of Law. "These cards are really quite extraordinary. You don't have any clue as to their origins?"

She shook her head. "I think—I think the right thing to do is to take them to one of the gods' shrines," she said softly.

He raised his eyebrows. Her voice was filled with something complex, but he could not decipher what it was. He set the cards carefully back in the box, closed the lid and set the box respectfully back onto the mantel.

"I am no expert in items of Power, but if you are unsure about these, then offering them to the gods at one of the shrines would be appropriate." He turned to put his hand on her shoulder, spreading his fingers over the finely sculpted shape of it, gently rubbing her through the soft cloth of her tunic. Giving in to temptation, he said quietly, "I have a very selfish desire to fall asleep listening to your voice. Can I coax you into reading to me for a little while?"

She swallowed and told him huskily, "I would be glad to."

His conscience stirred and grumbled. She had done so much for him already. He squashed it, choosing the selfish act, choosing to explore everything he could with her. He wanted to hear her voice. She had agreed.

Experience told him that she certainly knew how to say no. He could not both hunt her and simultaneously protect her from himself.

He walked into the shadowed bedroom, drew off his robe and laid it at the foot of the bed, and slid naked between the sheets. As the cool linen slid across his skin, an image came to him of Xanthe, spread underneath his body, her face tilted up in agonized pleasure, and as tired as he was, his penis stiffened again and throbbed with urgency.

He ignored it. Now was not the time to act. As disconcerted as Xanthe had shown herself to be over the attraction that grew between them, he suspected it was too soon for her. He did not want to initiate anything prematurely. They each deserved better.

A chair scraped across the floor. He called out, "Why don't you leave it? There is more than enough room for you to sit on the bed."

A pause, then she said, "Very well."

He lit the lantern on the bedside table while she shut and bolted the cottage door. By the time she stepped into the room, he lay back on the pillows with the covers pulled up to his chest. He watched her from underneath lowered eyelids as she moved to the pile of books. Her long body moved with a grace that caught at his throat. He longed to touch her with reverence and tell her how much she was coming to mean to him.

"Which book would you like for me to read?" she asked.

"I don't care," he told her. "Why don't you pick one that you're interested in?"

"All right." She hesitated then chose a Dark Fae story and settled on one corner of the bed, leaning back against the headboard with one leg bent and tucked underneath her.

He closed his eyes as she began to read. The liquid notes of her voice filled the room, shaping words that created a story, but he did not care about that. He merely listened to the sound of her voice, the intonation and inflection, and the cadence she gave to each sentence, as if he was listening to a solo musician. It was incredibly soothing.

She halted, faltering into silence, as he turned onto his side and nuzzled her thigh, resting one relaxed hand on her knee. He refused to pull away or regret the move, and after a pause she resumed the story, her voice much softer.

After a few moments more, a light, gentle weight came down on the back of his head. She rested her hand on him as she read.

Naida had not been affectionate. They had maintained separate bedrooms, coming together for sex but never sleeping in the same bed. He had accepted that about her. Some people simply weren't.

He was affectionate.

He smiled and slipped into a doze.

Sometime later, he roused as the bed shifted and Xanthe began to ease away. Without really thinking about it, he tightened his hand on her knee, murmuring, "Stay."

She drew in a quick breath, the slight sound seemed loud in the silence of the bedroom. She said softly, "I thought you had fallen asleep."

"I did. You moved." His voice was gravelly.

"I'm sorry I woke you."

He yawned and rolled onto his back, then opened his eyes to look at her. She wore an uncertain, vulnerable expression that squeezed at his chest. She would never be one for the cynical dalliances that the nobility indulged in. He lifted his hand to her, she took it and he pressed her fingers.

He told her quietly, "The bed is large, and there is more than enough room for two. You could even sleep with the covers between us if you like. No matter what you may have been used to in the past, I would feel better knowing that you weren't on the cold hard floor, but it is entirely up to you. I don't want you to be uncomfortable in any way."

She was silent for so long. As he waited, he urged her, *do it. Choose to do what you really want.*

At last she whispered, "I'll stay."

Tension had gathered in his limbs as he waited for her to decide. At her words it released, leaving a lingering lightness that felt like joy. He slid over as she shrugged out of her trousers, revealing long, gorgeous pale legs. Without looking at him, she lifted the top quilt and slipped into bed, leaving the sheet and a cotton blanket as a privacy barrier between them. The last thing she did was blow out the lamp before she settled with a sigh.

He kept his breathing soft and even, even as desire flooded his body.

Then she said in entirely prosaic exasperation, "Rats. We should have eaten up the rest of the clotted cream at supper, and I forgot all about it."

He lay frozen for a moment, all thought suspended. When he burst out laughing, she chuckled too.

He rolled over, and despite the barrier between them, he pulled her into his arms and hugged her. She came willingly, fitting herself to him, one arm tucked around him as he guided her head onto his shoulder. He pressed his lips to her forehead, lingering over the caress and stroked her still damp hair. She nuzzled at his bare shoulder, breathing deeply as she settled and, muscle by muscle, relaxed.

Holding her gave him a feeling of incredible rightness, comfort and relief. When he slept, for the first time in a very long time, there was no pain.

WHEN HE OPENED his eyes again, it was full morning and he was alone. Disappointed, he laid a hand on the pillow she had used. It was still warm. She had only just left the bed.

His body had the memory of holding Xanthe through the night. At one point, she curled onto her side and he moved too, curling behind her to spoon with her, one arm wrapped around her waist. She had laced her fingers through his as he buried his nose in her soft, silken hair.

Now she moved around in the other room. The quiet sounds were already comforting and familiar. Cautiously he tried a full body stretch. The muscles in his back still gave a twinge, but the warning no longer seemed filled with dire consequences. He should start some exercises today.

He rose out of bed, reveling in the sense of his returning strength, and slipped on a clean pair of trousers. Then he left the bedroom to commence stalking the woman he meant to make his lover.

She knelt at the hearth, laying wood for a morning fire. Her hair was loose and tousled, and her cheek was creased from the pillow linens—and there, it happened again. She had grown even more beautiful to him.

I'm falling in love with you, he thought. *And damn, it's a deep, deep fall.*

Falling in love with her wasn't a decision; it was a full mind-body, transformative experience. Backing away, choosing not to explore the opportunity—that would the decision. And he wasn't about to throw any of this away. It was too rare, too enriching. She was too fine of a treasure to be so disregarded.

Besides, he hungered for her, for everything she was. For her dedication and loyalty, for the sensuality of her long, lithe body, for the fullness of emotion he caught shimmering in her eyes when she looked at him.

She straightened and pushed the hair out of her face

in a self-conscious gesture as he walked over to her. He pulled her into his arms, tilted up her face and kissed her. Not a quick kiss this time, but a slow, searching explorative caress.

His lips remembered the shape of hers and were eager to mold to them again, while his heart thundered and his entire body hardened, and he felt immersed in a coursing river of emotion, in her. Breathing deeply, he fisted one hand in her hair, wanting to deepen the kiss but waiting for some kind of sign.

Kiss me. Kiss me back.

Her arms came around him, hands flattening greedily against his back even as she pulled her head away. She muttered, "We shouldn't be doing this—"

He flashed back fiercely, "Fuck that."

He never cursed. The shock of it bolted across her face. Then he realized how tightly his hand had clenched in her hair. He willed himself to pry his fingers open, to loosen his hold and stroke her hair gently. His hand was unsteady.

She stared at him, her gaze clear open down to the bottom of her soul.

"Xanthe," he said between his teeth as a horrible thought occurred to him. "Have you made promises to someone else?"

Her expression turned even more shocked. "No!"

"Then if you say a word about me being the Chancellor or you being a guard, I might just throttle you. There is no place for that here, between us. I am just a man who wants to kiss you. Do you want to kiss me back? That is the only consideration of any relevance in this moment. If you do not, just say so and I'm sorry I assumed too much—"

She lunged up on tiptoe, her arms snaking around his neck, and kissed him hard.

There it was, what he had been looking for, her full-bodied, full-hearted cooperation. He closed his eyes and sank into her mouth, spearing into her as deeply as he could go.

What they created together was a wild storm of emotion. This time when she pulled back, she was shaking all over.

He *loved* that.

"Okay," she whispered. "Okay."

He was not prepared to let her off the hook. He cupped the nape of her neck, holding her in place as he leaned his forehead on hers. He said in a low voice, "You will stay in the bed again with me tonight."

She licked her lips and said, "Yes."

He pressed her further, one hand gripping her hip. "And there will not be a sheet or a blanket between us."

Her dark gaze searched his. Her eyes were such a lovely, deep color, filled with clarity, intelligence and depth. "No blankets, Aubrey." Her fingertips stroked over his lips. "Except for the ones we pull over us both."

He released a long, pent-up breath and pressed a kiss against her fingers.

She shook her head. "You have knocked everything

sensible outside of my head again. I think I was starting to fix breakfast."

He purred, "We could always go back to bed right now."

She lost all of her composure again. "I—you—seriously?"

He laughed, a throaty, delighted sound. She sounded almost panicked at the thought. "Forget about breakfast, or even bed right now. Why don't we step outside for some fresh air. We could even go for a walk. The river is close, isn't it?"

She took a step back to eye him, her gaze turning assessing. She smiled. "You're really doing better."

He nodded. "I'm still stiff, especially in my back. But it's much better now."

"An oiled massage would help with a lot of that stiffness."

That demon of lunacy took over his tongue. He said, deadpan, "I think an oiled massage would take care of all kinds of stiffness."

Hot color washed over her cheeks. She added, strangled, "Certainly, that is, if you—think you might—I meant especially on that wound on your back to loosen up the muscles."

He shouted with laughter. "By all the gods, woman, how did you survive in the army for so long?"

Her embarrassment turned into a glare. "I'm not like this with anybody else!"

His laughter faded. Warmed, he cupped her cheek

and rubbed his thumb over those soft, unusually full lips. "Really?"

She nodded dumbly.

"I cherish all of it," he whispered.

Clearly she was not used to compliments, for she showed none of the polished deflection practiced by so many of the ladies of his acquaintance. Every word he said affected her deeply; he could see it in her eyes.

She was an assassin, and she had survived not only in Urien's palace for decades, but she had also survived Thruvial's household. Yet with him, she did not barrier any part of herself or use the many tools that must exist in her repertoire. Instead she revealed to him a heart of glass, fragile and beautifully faceted in every way, luminous with light.

He could not remember ever feeling so touched, or so honored.

"Come," she said. "I'll show you my favorite spot by the river. We can even fish if you want. I like fish for breakfast."

"So do I," he told her.

He got dressed fully, pulling on a shirt and boots. The day was fine enough again that no jacket was necessary. He tied his hair back with the leather strip, and splashed his face with water from the basin.

She had braided back her hair and gathered a basket of fishing supplies from a bottom shelf. As soon as he gave her a nod, she lifted her sword and harness from the hook by the door, although she did not bother to shrug it on.

He took the basket so it would free one of her hands then he captured it with his own, lacing his fingers through hers. Giving him a gleaming, bright smile, she led him on a pleasant walk to the river.

Their route bisected a large path that was more of a small road that followed the river's length. Now that he knew where the river was, he knew the path would lead to Adriyel, but he no longer cared to follow it. They settled in the shade of a massive oak tree.

Adriyel was the great river in the Dark Fae land. It poured hundreds of leagues through the heart of the land. The bank on the opposite side was certainly visible, but the details were obscured in the distance. It was treacherous to swim the long length from one side to the other, but every year some fools attempted it. Many were swept downstream and drowned.

Here, down a steep bank from the oak, there was an indentation with a relatively shallow pool. Smiling, she pointed down to it. "This was my favorite place in the heat of the summer, although my father never took his eyes off of me for a moment, for fear I would forget and get too close to the river's current."

"This must have been a great place to play as a child," he said.

"It was. We were happy." She lifted a shoulder. "I remember us being happy, at any rate. I'm sure he missed my mother, but she died in childbirth with me, so I never knew her. He was my only parent as a child growing up."

That would have made losing him especially hard for her. Dark Fae could live for a very long time, but there were still accidents, war and certain diseases that could claim lives. Long, long ago, his own parents had been taken in a virulent epidemic that had swept through their home seat in the country.

She sprawled with her long legs crossed at the ankle. He braced himself against the trunk of the oak to go through a round of stretching exercises. She watched closely, and offered some suggestions. Afterward, he lay beside her on the thick, rich grass of the bank, hands laced behind his neck as they talked.

Neither bothered to reach for the fishing basket. They were too focused on each other to care. The sunlight turned the green oak leaves golden, and a fresh cool breeze blew off river. Sexual arousal and affection blanketed them together in warmth and comfort, and imbued him with a sense of wellbeing.

They both heard the voices at the same time.

Male voices, approaching in their direction.

"It must be around here somewhere," said one. "This is the area they said. Just a bit further, maybe around that bend."

"Well, we've got to continue," said another. "There's no going back now."

Even as Aubrey sat up, Xanthe threw herself on him, one hand clamped over his mouth. She stared into his eyes, her own gaze sharp and steady.

"Don't make a sound," she told him telepathically.

He nodded as he clasped her wrist. *"I understand."*

"I am going to check where they are." She rolled off him and to her feet in one silent, lithe movement, scooping up her sword and harness as she rose. She shrugged it on quickly, her expression as keen as the blade that settled between her shoulders. She glanced down at him and touched a finger to her lips. He nodded again, and she disappeared through the waist high grass that bordered the path.

He rolled to his feet, not nearly as gracefully as she, as his wretched back muscles threatened to seize up again. After a second's consideration, he snatched up the fishing basket, not because the contents mattered so much as leaving it on the bank would have given away their presence. When he noticed the indentation their bodies had made in the grass, he wiped the area back and forth with one boot until the marks were gone.

By then Xanthe was back. She had drawn her sword. She gestured to him with her free hand. *"Come on, we must go this way."*

She led him on a different, more difficult route than they had taken earlier, further upstream for a while before they cut back across the path, and through a tangled, overgrown thicket, until finally they arrived back at the cottage.

As soon as they stepped inside, she grabbed her wrist guards that held throwing knives and began to strap them on.

"I need to follow them and discover what they're up to," she said, in a rapid, quiet voice. "It's possible their presence doesn't have anything to do with us, but we need to know if they're hunting you. As soon as I leave, I want you to bolt the door and the windows. Don't answer if anyone knocks. There are the kitchen knives if you need weapons. I'll return as fast as I can."

"Don't do this," he said. He grabbed her by the shoulders.

She stared at him as if he were crazy. "I have to."

"Then I'll come with you." He glared around the cottage. "Gods damn it, there's only one sword."

"Of course there's only one sword. You are not yet healed enough to face another fight."

"No one will refrain from attacking me because I'm not yet healed enough to face it," he snapped. "I can hold my own if I have to."

"Aubrey, listen to me." Her face was fierce. "In this one thing there is no equity between us. There is only one person in the world like you, and there are dozens like me. You are the Chancellor. I am your guard. I swear to you, I will be back."

Her words struck him like individual blows. He grabbed her and spun her around to face him, his fingers digging into her shoulders.

"No, you listen to me," he said between his teeth. "I will not let you go out there alone. I will not remain tamely in this cottage and wait for you, without knowing whether or not you are all right, or if you may have been killed. There is no one else in the world like you, and I will not run the risk of losing you just after I found you. We go together or we stay here. Together. Either way, you choose, but that's the only choice you're going to get."

Chapter Seven

Love

SHE STARED UP at him, mesmerized by the taut emotion that transformed his expression and clenched his long body. His hands felt hard as iron as his fingers dug into her shoulders, but she paid no attention to the discomfort. All she could do was hear the echo of his words resounding in her head.

"There is no one else in the world like you."

"I will not run the risk of losing you just after I found you."

He sounded—he sounded like he might—

By sheer force of will, she yanked herself back to the only thing that was relevant. She hissed, "I will not let anyone hurt you again, ever."

He said, "You said yourself their presence probably doesn't have anything to do with us. And if they are hunting for us, they will find the cottage soon enough."

"Not if I find them first." She raised her hands and tried to knock away his hold, but she refused to strike him hard, and he refused to let go of her. "If they are hunting for you—if they find the cottage, they can pin us in here."

He shook her, not hard but tightly enough to snap her attention back to his face. "Stop reacting and think," he said, still in that harsh-edged voice. "Nobody knows I'm here, just you, Tiago and Niniane and they would never breathe a word to anyone, yes?"

Her breath came hard. After a moment, she said, "Yes."

Although his features had calmed somewhat, the tension had not left his body. He pushed her backward until she came up against the wall. He said softly, "So the only way anyone could possibly think to look here is through the wildest chance that either Tiago or Niniane let slip some very specific information. Yes?"

She didn't know where he was going with this, but she was pretty sure she didn't like it. She snapped, "Yes."

He pushed his body against hers and rested his forearms on the wall on either side of her head, pinning her. Then he put his forehead to hers.

If he had been an enemy, she knew exactly what she would do to get away. A knee to the groin and a hard clip over the head with both hands locked together. That would buy her enough space and time to draw her sword.

But he wasn't the enemy. He was the dearest thing in the world to her. Even the thought of doing violence to him caused her to feel slightly queasy.

"I'm willing to take that wildest chance and stay here with you," he said. "I am not willing to take that wildest chance and let you go alone into a situation that might be deadly for you."

Somehow her arms ended up around his waist. She held him in a clinch. "I cannot stay safe and guard you at the same time."

"You're fired," he said immediately. He lowered his head and nuzzled her.

She felt like she was nearly leaping out of her skin with so many conflicting impulses. "You can't fire me." Her voice was all over the place, wildly unsteady. "I don't work for you."

"I am close friends with your employers. You're fired as soon as they come back." His lips brushed her cheek. "Xanthe, stay with me."

She took fistfuls of his shirt, feeling the broad, tight muscles underneath. "I am not willing to take the wildest chance on your safety and wellbeing either."

"I know, darling." He kissed the indentation at the corner of her mouth. "Everything you have done for days has been for my best good." He lifted his head slightly. His expression had turned tender. "No one has ever cared for me like you have."

"No one ever will." The words escaped her; they just escaped her, barely audible and yet laying her soul wide open.

He tilted his head and covered her mouth hard with his, a strong, confident taking that pushed her head back against the wall. Her legs shook; she felt drenched with erotic shock as he deepened the kiss, pushing into her mouth with his tongue. She could barely breathe and couldn't think. Her body's instincts took over and she kissed him back wildly.

His hardened lips slid over hers, slick with their moisture. Her heart was pounding so that she thought it might burst from her chest. She was almost lost, almost—

But no. Decades of training asserted itself.

She yanked her mouth away and gasped, "I need to know where those men went."

He was breathing as heavily as she was, his entire body run through with the finest tremor. He stared at her mouth, his darkened gaze sensual and compulsive. For a moment she thought he would refuse to lift his body weight from hers. Then with a grimace, he pulled back. "All right. We go together."

She didn't try to argue anymore—with their last fierce exchange they had catapulted each other into a strange new realm where she didn't understand the rules. Instead she shrugged out of her harness and tried to hand her sword to him. "Take this. I'll take the knives."

He stared down at the sword in her hand without moving to take it. Then he gave her a quirk of a smile. "When I am up to speed, I am a perfectly good swordsman. But I am not at my best, and you have to be one of the finest in the army for Tiago to agree to you becoming one of Niniane's guards. You keep the sword. I'll take the knives."

She scowled, not liking either possibility for how

they divided the weapons. But she strapped the harness back on again, while he took her wrist guards with the knives. Then they slipped quietly out of the cottage, into the growing heat of the day.

Sunshine pressed down heavily, the silence broken with the occasional call from birds and the heavy drone of insects. Aubrey gestured for her to lead the way, and she took them in a wide circle that circumvented the cottage. Having found no sign of the men, they moved wider afield until they checked the path where the men had been before. Then finally they moved to the bank of the river. She was studying the bank for footprints when Aubrey nudged her gently and pointed downstream.

She glanced where he pointed. Some distance away the riverbank jutted out in a small promontory that was little more than a tangled mass of tree trunks and debris that had been swept downstream. A small barge had gotten tangled in the debris, and two men, covered in mud, were working to get it loose.

The knot of tension that had tightened her shoulders loosened.

Aubrey slipped an arm around her shoulders from behind, his forearm crossing at her collarbones. He pulled her back against him and said in her ear, "Looks like someone's livelihood might have slipped its mooring and floated downstream. Satisfied?"

She nodded, letting her head fall back against his shoulder. After a moment, she said, "I'm not sorry for being so paranoid. You really did almost die."

He heaved a rough sigh. "I know."

His body felt hot and tense. Her mind was split wide open with incredulity for this blaze of fire that had leapt up between them.

"There is no one else in the world like you. I'm willing to take that wildest chance and stay here with you."

He cupped her neck with one hand while he kissed the sensitive shell of her ear and whispered, "Let's go home."

Home? The sound of that word, coming from him, gave her another thrill of shock. Unable to form words, she nodded. His arm loosened and he let her go.

They made short work of the trip back to the cottage. Once there, she shrugged out of her harness and hung her sword on its hook. Aubrey gazed at her steadily while he yanked open the fastenings on the wrist guards. Her mind hazed with heat. Desire for this man was the sweetest pain she had ever known. That he might grow to want her too was beyond anything she could have dreamed of, extraordinary.

In fact it was hardly believable.

The thought drove her across the room, away from him. She wrapped her arms around her middle, chewing on her lip as she looked guiltily at the box on the fireplace mantle. His slow, measured tread came up behind her; she was so hyperaware of him, she knew to the exact moment when his hands would come down on her shoulders.

"What's wrong?" he asked quietly.

The question burst out of her. "Do you think the gods can make us do things we wouldn't otherwise do?"

His thumbs rubbed soothingly at her shoulder blades. "Why do you ask?"

Her body was trembling with the force of her own desire to keep silent, to take what he offered her with his hands and his mouth. But she couldn't.

She whispered, "When Dr. Telemar—the medusa—couldn't identify what kind of Power was in those Tarot cards, I started to wonder about those old legends about the gods putting items in the world to enact their will. Inanna's card keeps surfacing. If the cards are hers—could they be influencing us to act in ways we might not otherwise act?"

He was silent for a long, thoughtful moment. Then he brushed her braid aside and pressed a kiss to the nape of her neck. "The chances of such a thing would be outrageously rare, you know," he said gently. "And while the good Dr. Telemar is no doubt highly proficient at her job, she is but one physician and the world is filled with many strange and different magics."

"I know," she whispered.

He pulled her into his arms. "Even if we were so lucky to have an item of Inanna's working in our lives, no, I do not believe the gods can or would make us act against our natures or inclinations. Our free will is one of the primal Powers after all. Inanna may give us the opportunity for love, but it's our choice whether or not we take that opportunity, and love is what we make of it."

She said in a low voice, "I just find it hard to believe that you might—you might want me."

He turned her around and stared into her eyes. "Xanthe, you are the most beautiful surprise in my life. I hardly noticed you at first. You carry the quiet of a river with a still surface that runs very deep. I found that the more I looked at you, the more I saw—and now the more I see of you, the more beautiful you become and the more I want you." He paused then said deeply, "I've never wanted anyone the way I have grown to want you."

Her trembling deepened as she listened to him. Overcome, she laid her hand against his lean cheek. "Me neither."

He smiled at her, slow and intimate, as his hands drifted gently, gently to the front of her shirt. He gave her plenty of time to say something, to object or pull away, as he teased open the top button, then a second one. Her breathing quickened as she watched his long, clever fingers work the material open. When she glanced up at him, she saw that his breathing had quickened also.

Her shirt came unfastened and he pulled the edges open, gazing down at her breasts. She was slim everywhere, muscles sleek and strong under pale, smooth skin. Her breasts were high and slight, the pale pink nipples pebbling in the open air.

He touched the swelling, velvet soft skin of her breast with shaking, gentle hands, and brushed the extremely sensitive jut of one nipple with the back of his fingers. Sensation and emotion coursed through her, the small pleasure brought to an extreme by the awareness that he was the one who touched her with such care.

She looked up at his dear face, both noble and kind, and surprised an expression of vulnerability. He said, very low, "I have not been with anyone since my wife died. I've felt dead inside for so long."

Compassion wrenched her. She circled his wrists loosely with her hands. "We don't have to do this, Aubrey, if you're not ready."

"Yes, we do." His eyes blazed. "She took so much from me. I will not lose any more of my life to her. For a long time, I didn't see how I could learn to trust someone again. Until you."

Tears burned at the back of her eyes. "I would never hurt you. Never. I'll kill anyone who tries."

His clenched expression softened into a tender smile. He cupped her face and whispered, "I believe you."

She pulled his hair loose from the tie that held it back, and the long raven strands fell about his lean face as he bent his head to kiss her. Starting out light and tender, the caress rapidly escalated until he gripped the back of her head and dug, groaning, into her open, inviting mouth.

Need for him throbbed low in her body. She pulled at his shirt until the buttons scattered across the floor then ran her hands hungrily across his hard, lean chest. He snaked an arm around her and yanked her against him, until they were hip to hip. As she felt the full length of his erection against her pelvis, she made an animal noise and rubbed against him.

Still kissing her, he pushed her, back and back, and she obeyed blindly until she came up against the table. He nudged her to sit and he tore off the rest of her clothes while she yanked his trousers open and reached greedily for his penis. It was hard, thick and beautifully made, silken skin stretched over stiffened flesh. Staring at his face, she fingered the length of his cock and stroked him, while he closed his eyes and swallowed hard. He pushed at her hands with his hips, and she pumped him slowly, losing herself in the moment of giving him pleasure.

His voice turned guttural, he said, "Stop."

She muttered a protest as he pulled out of her grip, and she reached for him again, but he brushed her seeking hands out of the way and pushed her back onto the table. Once she understood what he wanted, she lay back, her spine arched and torso stretched out on display for him as her legs spilled over the edge.

He froze, one hand planted on the table beside her waist, breathing hard as he stared down at her. Some strong emotion played over his face. Worried, she reached up to touch his lips. "What is it?"

He whispered from the back of his throat, "It just happened again. You're even lovelier than ever."

She could tell there was no barrier in him anywhere. He looked at her, totally bared and open, and she knew what he meant, for he had never looked so beautiful to her. She murmured, "Come inside."

He shook his head. "Not yet. Soon."

He came down over her, resting his weight on his elbows as he traced the line of her collarbone with his tongue. His heartbeat thudded hard and fast against her breast. She hooked her heels on the on the edge of the table, cradling him between her legs and murmuring incoherently as she stroked his hair. It was impossible to love him more than she did, impossible. Tears slipped from the corners of her eyes and soaked into her hair as he worked his way down to her breasts. Eyes closed, he suckled first at one nipple then the other, teasing her sensitive flesh lightly and then drawing hard, so that her clitoris throbbed in agonizing response and she cried out, clawing at his shoulders in urgent, wordless demand.

Still suckling, he worked one hand between their bodies and fingered the soft petals of her sex, drawing out moisture and rubbing his cock against her. She was so slick with arousal, she felt the wetness coating him.

He pushed steady and gentle until the thick, broad head of his penis slipped in, and he stopped just long enough that she pulled at his hair and sobbed out, "Don't tease me right now."

At that he threw back his head. His face was twisted; he looked transformed, outside of himself. A growl wrenched out of him, and in one convulsive move he sheathed himself inside of her.

In, in, in, he was all the way in. She cried out,

gripping him tightly with her inner muscles, while she raised her legs and wrapped them around his torso.

His hoarse, panting breath was like a bellows in her ear, and his long hair covered her face. He shook all over. She hugged him with her whole body and soul, fiercely, stroking the back of his head with one hand while she rubbed his back.

"Tell me you're all right," she whispered, growing anxious as he held so still.

Tell me you won't regret this.

He looked down at her and smiled, his face filled with tenderness and sharp passion. He said, "I've never been better. You feel like a wet silken fist. Gods—Xanthe—"

She tightened on him harder as he slid out, and he shuddered hard and drove back in. He pulled out again, excruciatingly slow. Unable to wait, she mewled and thrust her hips up, impaling herself on him. His big body jerked as he gasped. He put a hand between them again; she felt him probing for her clitoris as he fucked her. Something came out of her mouth, an uncontrolled string of words. She had no idea what she said. She was on fire everywhere, everywhere. It blazed from the point of his entry, the unbearably gorgeous pressure of his fingers on exactly the right place.

"Oh shit," he said.

He twisted in her arms. Inside, she felt him begin to pulse as he lost control. Then that desire, that sweetest pain she felt for no one but him, peaked like a starburst.

She cried out as her own climax rippled through her. He ground against her, shuddering.

Silence, their passion released. She cradled him as he rested his forehead on her shoulder. The table was uncomfortably hard on her spine, and she would not have moved for the world. With her fingers, she circled the slight knob of bone at the base of his nape and traced what she could reach of the long line of scar across his back, soaking up every sensual piece of evidence she could get of him.

I'll not ever forget this moment, she thought. *Not ever, not even if I live for a very, very long time.*

EVENTUALLY THE DISCOMFORT of his position forced him to move. He pushed himself up on one hand, wincing as his back muscles seized up in protest and his softened penis slid out of her.

"Well, this is inelegant," he said through gritted teeth.

The gorgeous dazed look left her face, and she laughed, her gaze sympathetic. "It's that damn wound on your back, isn't it?"

He nodded. Limber and graceful, she slid out from underneath him and rolled off the table. When she was upright, she slipped under his arm and took his weight, helping him to straighten. He forced himself to take a deep breath. Then he kissed her.

She murmured, and he drew her close, relishing the feel of her naked body against his. At last, with obvious reluctance, she pulled away. "Let me get the vial of oil," she said. "You need a back massage to loosen those muscles, especially after the stretching exercises from earlier and—you know." Unexpectedly, her face turned dark red.

"I won't say no," he said. He stroked her cheek, inexpressibly delighted at the blush. Delighted with everything about her. "Xanthe, I love you."

She grew very still, her eyes, full of that great, shining heart of glass, fixed on him. When she made as if to say something, he touched her lips with two fingers and shook his head with a smile. Just because he felt the need to tell her how he felt didn't mean that she should feel the need to reciprocate.

He went into the other room and eased down onto the bed to lay on his aching back with a muffled groan. A few moments later, she joined him.

He loved watching her walk across the room nude. Her breasts were reddened by his attention, and the black silken triangle between her legs glistened with moisture. Her body was sleek and powerful, like a panther's, and despite the shyness she had shown to him in various other ways, she had no body shyness at all and she moved with complete, athletic confidence that he found incredibly sexy. His cock stirred as he watched her; he was so hungry for her, he was already beginning to stiffen again.

She had gathered up their clothes and she set them on the floor by the bed. Then she took a small vial of oil and poured some into the palm of her hand. Her gaze flew involuntarily to his groin, and he clenched his teeth on another laugh as she flushed pink all over.

"Oh gods, please do," he growled.

She scolded, "I'm supposed to rub your back!"

He loved it when she scolded him. He grasped her knee, gently. "My back is perfectly fine while I'm lying down. It can wait. It's everything else that feels urgent right now."

She looked at him, stricken laughter in her gaze, and he could see that she was tempted.

"After we work on your muscles a bit."

He gave her a lazy, one-sided, calculating smile. "Very well, but I won't roll over until you give me a kiss."

He watched her gaze grow heavy lidded, and his cock stiffened further. "All right."

She bent over him, her mouth softened, and he raised his head to meet her, kissing her lavishly, feeling hunger for her roar to a fever pitch all over again. When she would have pulled away, he grabbed her and yanked her back down, so that she overbalanced and fell on him.

Instinctively she caught herself on his chest, bracing on the hand that had held the palm full of oil. The warm liquid splashed across his torso as her slippery hand slid off his skin, and she sprawled on top of him.

He growled deeper, an arm wrapped around her neck as he plunged hectically between her lips. While he fucked her mouth with his tongue, he rubbed his chest with a hand until it was slick with oil, then he palmed her breast, that high, firm luscious mound of flesh. She moaned, the shaken sound vibrating in his mouth.

The oiled, slick friction of their bodies drove him out of his mind. He bit her neck, suckled at her ear, sank both fists into her hair and muttered, "Climb on top."

The glazed look was back in her eyes, arousal shimmering out of her flesh in waves of velvet heat. He held her by the hair down to him, while she straddled his hips with hers. She groped for his cock blindly; when she took hold of him, she brought his tip to her entrance and sank down, down, sheathing him again in that tight, wet fist.

She was off balance, bent over, her weight on her elbows, but he could not seem to make his fingers loosen from her hair. It was uncivilized, possessive in the extreme. It was either unlike him or it was the truest manifestation of who he was becoming with her.

He hissed against her lips, "Fuck me, just like this."

She groaned and obeyed, her hips moving on him in a primitive rhythm that he met with upward thrusts, spearing into her with cock and tongue, blind to everything but the need to enter her, enter her. She sobbed for breath, the jagged puffs of breath against his face as erotic as anything they had done together.

Her face was reddened; tears streaked her eyes, and strands of her hair were plastered to her damp face and neck. "Gorgeous, gorgeous," he said into her mouth. "You gorgeous woman."

At that she gave a sharp cry, her whole body going taut as a bow, and he felt the ripple of her orgasm deep inside of her as she clenched on him. It sent him over the edge. He slid a hand down to her ass, pressing her down hard as he ejaculated deep inside of her. It satisfied everything primal inside of him.

The world pulsed with their heartbeats, their sweating bodies fused together. She lay across him, her head resting on his chest. Finally he was able to loosenhis grip on her hair. He pushed the strands back from her face and tried to smooth the tangles out.

"I've loved you for a very long time," she said. Her voice was very soft, almost inaudible. He stilled, straining to hear every word. "Of course mostly that was hero worship and not very realistic."

"I'm no hero," he said.

She snorted softly. "You're a hero to everyone, Aubrey. Just not to yourself." He frowned, but she was continuing. "Then I got to know you better. The real you. The real, cranky, kind, funny you. Gods help me."

He cupped her face. "Why do you need the gods to help you, darling?"

Her eyes were closed. She whispered, "We'll be going back to our lives soon enough."

His frown deepened. "Xanthe," he said tightly. "I don't know what this is for you, but this is not just an interlude for me. Yes, our time here at the cottage is outside the boundaries of normality, and yes, we have our jobs and duties waiting for us back in the city, but I am living an authentic life—who I am here is who I am back there too. I said I love you. I didn't say it because we just had sex. I said it because I love you. You had better tell me if you don't want to see me when we get back—and even then I'll try to persuade you otherwise—"

She rose up and kissed him quickly. "No, that's not what I meant! I—I didn't want to presume anything just because we—we—you know." She made a gesture that encompassed them and the bed.

His tightness eased. He smiled at her. "Please presume all the 'you knows' that you want. I strongly encourage all kinds of presuming from you."

That startled her into a grin. As she opened her mouth to say something—

They heard voices approaching the cottage: Niniane's and Tiago's.

Panic flashed across Xanthe's face. She rolled off the bed and peered out the window. "We didn't shut the cottage door," she muttered. She flew at her clothes.

While she yanked on her shirt and trousers, Aubrey rolled off the bed. He strolled over to the bedroom door to shut it firmly.

Just outside the cottage, Niniane called, "Hello, Aubrey? Xanthe? Are you here?"

He called out, "We're here, but we're not dressed. Give us a minute, and we'll be right out."

Silence. Then: "Okay."

He turned to Xanthe. "Darling, don't panic," he

whispered. "Take your time."

"She's only the Queen," Xanthe hissed. She dragged her fingers frantically through her hair and braided it. Apparently it wasn't straight enough to satisfy her, so she yanked it out and did it again. "And she's my employer. Oh holy gods, Tiago's out there."

He started to laugh as he dressed. When he slipped on his shirt, he couldn't find any buttons, so he left it open. Xanthe was still trying to get her hair into a plait when he opened the door and walked out.

Tiago stood in the doorway, facing the outside, arms crossed and harsh profile expressionless. Niniane stood by the table, unpacking canvas bags of supplies. She did not look expressionless. Her small, piquant face was full of suppressed glee.

"Hello," Aubrey said. "How are you today?"

"We are quite well," Niniane said. Her eyes danced. "You are looking so much better, Aubrey."

"I'm feeling better than I have in a long time," he told her, as he pressed a kiss to her cheek. He whispered, "Xanthe is in a panic. Tell Tiago to be nice or I will hurt him."

"Oh, he'll be nice," Niniane whispered back. "Or if he can't manage nice, he'll be silent if he knows what's good for him."

"I know what's good for me," Tiago said to the general out of doors.

Xanthe appeared, her back ramrod stiff. Her clothes were as neat as she could make them, and her braid was not quite immaculate, but really quite well done given the circumstances. She murmured, "Your grace, sir."

She was almost, but not quite, perfectly expressionless. Aubrey couldn't stand it. He walked over to her and put an arm around her. She just looked at him, her lips white. He was not altogether convinced that she was breathing.

We need to rip this bandage off right now, he thought. He said aloud, "Xanthe and I have just decided to continue seeing each other when we return to the city. We don't need your blessing, but we would very much appreciate it."

"Of course you have it," Niniane said immediately. She gave Xanthe a warm smile. "I couldn't be more delighted. I really mean that, Xanthe."

Aubrey felt the tension in Xanthe's shoulders ease, although she glanced at Tiago again. He did too. Tiago's eyebrows had raised, but other than that, for all intents and purposes he appeared to be watching birds.

"How is the investigation going?" Aubrey asked.

Tiago looked over one massive shoulder at Niniane who nodded. The Wyr lord said, "The investigation was over within twenty-four hours of your attack, with all arrests made."

At first the words didn't make sense. His arm fell from Xanthe's shoulders and he ran his fingers through his hair. "Wait a minute," he said. More like growled. "That would mean everything was over with the first time you came with supplies."

"That is correct," said Tiago.

Xanthe strode forward quickly, "Who did it?"

"Naida's father, Grove Ealdun, was behind it," Tiago said. "We have the people he hired too." He met Aubrey's gaze. "Your secretary, Sebrin, is a little battered around the edges but all right. Sebrin gave himself away when he went digging. Ealdun had captured him but hadn't yet killed him. When he realized you were responsible for sending Sebrin, he tried to have you killed, in part for revenge. In part, too, because he thought you were going to try to have him prosecuted for the false evidence. The ironic thing is that I don't think any of us would have bothered with prosecuting for the false evidence, but now of course it's attempted murder. The whole thing was pretty simple and straightforward, in a Dark Fae kind of way."

"You said there were complications," Aubrey snapped. He glared at Niniane, "You ordered me to stay here."

Niniane bit her thumbnail. She looked worried as she replied, "Neither one of us said there were complications with the investigation, Aubrey. We only said that there were complications."

"What does that mean?" he roared, fists on his hips.

Tiago gave him a warning look, but he ignored it

Niniane gave Xanthe an apologetic glance then said to him, "The night you were almost killed, I—saw something, Aubrey. I saw just how much you meant to Xanthe. So when Tiago tore through the investigation in record time, and he threw everybody in prison, well—you were here at the cottage anyway, so we just left you. This last year has been so hard on you both, each for your own reasons. I just wanted you to have a little time of peace and quiet together. I thought—I hoped you might find things to say to each other. I also knew neither one of you would say a word to each other outside of polite niceties in any other environment."

Xanthe said incredulously, "You were matchmaking?"

"Maybe," said Niniane. She offered them a smile. "A little. Plus, I know you, Aubrey Riordan." She shook a finger at him. "If you had been home, you would have started back to work much too early, despite doctor's orders. So I made you stay here with lots of fresh air, good food and nothing more strenuous than a few games and some good books."

Aubrey scrubbed his face with both hands. After a moment he started to laugh. "Okay," he said. "Okay."

"Are you mad at me?" Niniane asked. "I can't tell."

"I don't know," he said. He dropped his hands and looked at Xanthe, who appeared to feel about as uncertain as he did. "I don't think so. Mostly I'm grateful. As long as you don't mind," he said to Xanthe.

She shook her head. "I'm grateful too."

"See, I told you it would all work out," Niniane said to Tiago.

"You are, as always, perfectly right," Tiago told her.

TIAGO AND NINIANE stayed for a supper of grilled steaks, baked potatoes, salad greens and fresh pastries, and red wine. "You can come back home now, if you both want," Niniane said. She told Aubrey, "But if you do, you still can't go back to work for at least another sevenday."

He looked at Xanthe. "If I stay here, do I get to keep my nurse?"

Glee fizzed in Niniane's face. "Of course you do—that is, if she wants to stay too."

"Yes, Ma'am," said Xanthe, her lovely eyes smiling at Aubrey. "I would love to."

Niniane nodded. "Then that's settled."

Xanthe asked her, "How's Mouse, by the way?"

A shadow passed over Niniane's face and Aubrey frowned, bracing himself for bad news. "She's doing really well," Niniane said. "Her real name is Rachel. Her aunt and uncle have come to collect her, and they left for home yesterday."

"Why do you look sad?" he asked gently.

Niniane bit her lip as she stared at her plate. "I'm going to miss her."

Silence fell over the table. Children were, after all, rare enough gifts to the Elder Races. For Niniane and Tiago, the possibility of having children was nonexistent as long as she was Queen.

Aubrey set down his knife and fork as he looked around the table. Not so very long ago, he felt utterly bleak and betrayed, and so alone he would have welcomed death. Now sitting at the small table were the three people who meant the most to him. Blessings come in all ways, he thought, and they are always a surprise.

He raised his wine glass. “To new beginnings,” he said as he looked at Xanthe. Her gaze lit until she looked luminous. “And to peace.”

The others raised their glasses to clink with his.

Tiago said, “At least to peace for now.”

Epilogue

THE SEVEN SHRINES of the gods were scattered all over Adriyel. Inanna's shrine lay four days' ride from the city.

Xanthe and Aubrey took the trip several moons later when the leaves started to turn in the autumn. Travel was pleasant in the cool, quiet days, and the nights had not yet grown unpleasantly cold.

They argued the whole way, even as they drew near to their destination.

"I wish you would listen to me when I say that I am content," Xanthe said.

"You may be content, but I am not," he said. "I do not see why you won't marry me."

"It's not fitting," she said stubbornly.

"Xanthe, you are the biggest snob I have ever met." His face was grim, and he looked quite forbidding. She found it almost unbearably sexy.

She glared at him. "Unfair! You know very well the more traditionally minded nobility would shun you if you married a commoner." She grimaced. "They are every bit as snobbish as I am, if not more."

"Fuck them," he snapped.

She clapped a hand over her mouth, not wanting to laugh. It was always so shocking whenever he cursed. He did it so seldom.

He was continuing. "Seriously. I don't care if it turns me into a pariah. If anybody is going to judge us on the merits of being married to each other, I don't want to socialize with them anyway."

"You have a point," she admitted with reluctance. She blew out a frustrated breath. "But I don't know how to be anything except a guard or an assassin."

He gave her a heated glance. "And now my lover."

She could hardly look at him and stay upright on her horse. He rode with immaculate, confident grace.

When they had returned to Adriyel, she had resumed her duties as one of Niniane's attendants and he as Chancellor, but they spent every night together at his house, and when she had her two days off, they went together to the cottage. Nights had become a golden time of enchantment and intimacy. Some days she could barely wait until the sun had set.

She whispered, "And that."

They rode in silence. Then he told her, "You would make a perfectly ferocious wife."

She widened her eyes. "I know! I would never be able to stop guarding you. I would be a social calamity."

"Did you ever stop to think," he said between his teeth, "that I might actually want and need a perfectly ferocious wife and social calamity. That is why I keep proposing to you."

She scrubbed at her forehead. "You're not going to give up, are you?"

"The only thing I am going to give up are my guards."

Incredulity sliced at her. She pulled her horse to a stop. "You can't."

"I absolutely can." He pulled his mount to a halt as well. His expression had turned hard and ruthless, and damn him, it made him even sexier than ever. "My guards don't do anything but follow me around and doze in the hallways when I work. At any rate, that attack on me was an aberration and it happened moons ago. Besides, I've got to find a way to blackmail you somehow."

"What are you talking about?" she shouted.

His eyebrows rose. In that moment he actually looked haughty. "If you won't marry me, I won't keep my guards. End of subject."

She exploded. "That's the stupidest thing I've ever heard!"

He nudged his horse forward, a smile playing around the corners of his lips. "It is so satisfying to dig underneath that calm façade of yours. I think it has become my second favorite pastime, my most favorite being when we make love, of course."

He kicked his horse into a canter, and she followed. "Get back here!"

"Darling, it is no use arguing about this any further,"

he called over his shoulder. "You know I will do exactly as I say, and Niniane will be so angry at you if I dismiss my guards."

"Aubrey!" Sending her own horse into a gallop, she caught up with him easily. "You leave Niniane out of this."

He looked entirely ruthless. "In fact as soon as we return, I plan on telling her how unhappy your refusal makes me. Her sympathies will not lie with you on this, Xanthe. Not when you are free to marry me if you would only choose to do so."

That struck her into silence, as he had known it would, for as long as Niniane remained the Dark Fae Queen, she and Tiago might be mated but they could never marry. Xanthe fumed and brooded as they rode into a small valley that was dotted with copses of trees crowned with the fiery colors of autumn.

They found the shrine at a crossroads. It was a simple affair, a grotto built of ancient stone beside a bubbling spring. They tethered their horses. Xanthe dug into one of her packs to retrieve the box of Tarot cards which she had wrapped in protective silk. Aubrey held his hand out to her, and she took it. They walked together to the shrine.

It was a peaceful place, silent except for the constant play of water falling over stone, deep with a sense of greening life despite winter's approach. Others had left offerings before them, a withered bouquet of flowers, fruit that had been nibbled at by wildlife and scattered on the ground, a tiny pair of knitted baby shoes. The sight of those caught at Xanthe, and she blinked back a sudden impulse to tears as she sent up a silent prayer for that unknown baby.

"I want to think that those shoes were left in gratitude for the birth of a new baby," she said in a husky voice. "And not because some child has passed."

Aubrey rubbed her back and said gently, "Then that is what we will believe."

As she glanced at him, he nodded an encouragement to her. She walked over and laid the box in the grotto. The mellow Power of the cards bathed her hands one last time as she let them go. *Thank you,* she said silently to the goddess. Like a chalice, her heart was filled to the brim. She had not known she could hold so much emotion.

In this quiet, eternal place, her arguments against marriage seemed superfluous, especially since she was arguing against her own wishes. She turned to Aubrey. "Yes, I'll marry you."

His face lit with triumph and joy. "I knew it," he said. He pulled her into his arms.

"Don't be insufferable about it," she told him, smiling. She laid her head on his shoulder.

He held her, his face buried in her hair. "You are the love of my life," he whispered. "That means I get to be as insufferable as I like."

"Oh, is that what it means?" She laughed and he chuckled too. She turned her face into his neck, her arms wrapped around his waist.

They stood together for a while as peace soaked into their bones. Then Aubrey kissed her temple. "Are you ready to start back?"

"Yes." She pulled away, glanced at the shrine—and froze as her world tilted.

The silk wrapped box had vanished.

She managed to whisper, "Aubrey."

"What?" He followed the direction of her gaze and stood very still, his expression sharp with wonder. "I'll be damned. It was hers."

"I thought—I mean, I guess I didn't really think it was true. Like you said, the chances of it were outrageously rare." She felt like she was babbling but she couldn't seem to stop. "What do you suppose will happen to it now?"

"She'll cast it into the world someplace else," Aubrey said. "Who knows when, or where?"

Xanthe smiled. "How lovely."

Thank you!

Dear Readers,

Thank you for reading Hunter's Season! I hope you enjoyed the story!

Would you like to stay in touch and hear about new releases? You can:

- Sign up for my monthly email at: www.theaharrison.com
- Follow me on Twitter at @TheaHarrison
- Like my Facebook page at facebook.com/TheaHarrison

Reviews help other readers find the books they like to read. I appreciate each and every review, whether positive or negative.

Happy reading!
~Thea

Coming Soon:

The Wicked by Thea Harrison

For a librarian with a focus on rare magical books, Olivia's new job is a dream come true. She's been hired as part of a team to help manage the safe transportation of the collection of books owned by the Vampyre sorceress Carling Severan. The fact that the library is located on a mysterious island in an Other land only heightens the adventure.

Head of security for the expedition, Sebastian Hale is tired of his rootless life of adventure and finds himself attracted to the calm, beautiful librarian. But he's living a personal nightmare. He's been hit with a curse that is slowly taking away his sight, and he doesn't know if he'll survive the results.

But the powerful feelings growing between them, along with Sebastian's inner turmoil, take a backseat when they learn there's a traitor in their expedition team. With Elder Races politics and a priceless library on the line, they'll have to rely on each other to survive.

Look for these titles from Thea Harrison

THE ELDER RACES SERIES – FULL LENGTH NOVELS

Published by Berkley

Dragon Bound

Storm's Heart

Serpent's Kiss

Oracle's Moon

Lord's Fall

Kinked

Night's Honor

Midnight's Kiss

Shadow's End

MOONSHADOW TRILOGY

Moonshadow

Spellbinder

Lionheart *Early 2018

ELDER RACES NOVELLAS

True Colors

Natural Evil

Devil's Gate

Hunter's Season

The Wicked

Dragos Takes a Holiday

Pia Saves the Day

Peanut Goes to School

Dragos Goes to Washington

Pia Does Hollywood
Liam Takes Manhattan

GAME OF SHADOWS SERIES

Published by Berkley

Rising Darkness
Falling Light

ROMANCES UNDER THE NAME AMANDA CARPENTER

E-published by Samhain Publishing
(original publication by Harlequin Mills & Boon)
**These stories are currently out of print*

A Deeper Dimension
The Wall
A Damaged Trust
The Great Escape
Flashback
Rage
Waking Up
Rose-Coloured Love
Reckless
The Gift of Happiness
Caprice
Passage of the Night
Cry Wolf
A Solitary Heart
The Winter King

19060214R00091

Printed in Poland
by Amazon Fulfillment
Poland Sp. z o.o., Wrocław